TOY
SOLDIERS

Michael G. Keller

MONTAG

First Montag Press E-Book and Paperback Original Edition October 2016

Montag Press
ISBN: 978-1-940233-37-6
Editor - Nicholas Morine
Cover Illustrations © Garrett Kohanek
Jacket and book design © 2016 Niall Gray
Managing Director — Charlie Franco

A Montag Press Book
www.montagpress.com
Montag Press
1066 47th Ave. Unit #9
Oakland CA 94601 USA

Printed & Digitally Originated in the United States of America
10 9 8 7 6 5 4 3 2 1

"The clash of cultural identities is loud in this, Michael Keller's debut novel. Brash America – taut and monetized – locks horns with a tribal and anxious Africa, in a modern-day morality play that proves that identity is both nature and nurture. A machete-rattling ride that blends scenes of intense conflict with those of frustrated humanity. The ghost of Saul Bellow's Henderson looks down and shakes his head."

— David Mathew, author of *Sick Dice* and *O My Days*

"Keller's remarkable debut shows us what horrors flower from the seeds of Western greed. *Toy Soldiers* deftly transitions between the worlds of Manhattan hedge fund professionals and impoverished Congolese villagers, and through its characters' bloody conflicts — and heartfelt relations — we understand not only the consequences of actions but the interconnectedness of all human beings. This is a book that skillfully slices away the fat of the American ego."

— David Massengill, author of *Red Swarm*

"A brilliant American financial analyst is given a dangerous task. He travels far away and amidst the horrors which take place in rebel-held Congo, he discovers the depth of his own humanity. A great, well-written novel."

— Marcin Dolecki, author of *Philosopher's Crystal*

To Mom and Dad

1

The Jupiter Fund building dominated the southern shore of Manhattan like a gleaming blade cutting into the sky. At the apex was a flagpole, bearing no nation's colors – just a skull and crossbones whipping in the wind.

The nerve center at the top was a bustling, circular trading floor, packed with monitors displaying securities charts, news feeds, tickers and an avalanche of data and video flooding in from all over the world. Traders banged away at computers, barked into headsets and reaped money from global markets with efficiency and controlled aggression. A small army of assistants scurried around in fear, attending to their every whim.

The traders had a dirty reputation – their competitors at genteel, white-shoe firms saw them as sociopaths with Ivy League pedigrees. They had been hit with every allegation under the sun – insider trading, price manipulation, corporate espionage – but nothing stuck, because they always did right by their investors and the Securities and Exchange Commission had no teeth. They wore their accusations as badges of honor, as proof that they were pushing themselves to the very edge of legality, that they were using every last weapon in their arsenal to generate outsized returns.

Jupiter Capital Management dealt in "distressed assets" – the stock of near bankrupt companies and the high yielding debt of impoverished nations on the brink of collapse. In the common parlance, it was a "vulture fund," opportunistically circling over other people's misery and swooping in to peck apart the carcasses of dead institutions. When the traders smelled blood, they all pounced at once. They sniped each other and jockeyed for position, to establish dominance and grab the largest share of the spoils.

Milos Sterling surveyed his fiefdom from a glass office over-looking the trading floor. He had launched the fund decades prior and made his fortune several times over. Another billion here or there no longer affected on his lifestyle. He kept hunting because it was hard-wired in his limbic system. When his reptilian brain sensed weakness, he was conditioned to pounce. But perhaps the thrill was gone.

As a young man, Milos felt most alive dodging Soviet tanks that invaded his native Czechoslovakia. That was how he learned that disaster brought opportunity. He had actually struggled as a merchant in the halcyon days before his homeland was torn apart, but thrived when the Russian occupation created unnatural im-balances and shortages in basic necessities. Milos found that with boldness and cunning, he could realize immense profits in black markets. He provided necessities people once took for granted – an angel with an angle.

But one couldn't operate in these lucrative grey areas for long without getting pinched. Rather than facing down a short-ened, brutish life of hard labor in some frosty Siberian gulag, Mi-los sold out to the Soviets. He collaborated, kicked back bribes and informed on his own people, in exchange for license to keep plying his racket. Very few knew of this checkered past.

Milos Sterling still cut a handsome figure in his winter years, silver haired and always dressed in the finest tailored, Savile Row suits.

His crinkly eyes squinted at a commotion in a corner of the trading floor. Several of his wolves had worked themselves into a frenzy over what they saw on their monitors.

The intercom buzzed and a secretary spoke in hushed, urgent tones. "Excuse me, sir. Roger says he needs to see you."

"Send him in," Milos uttered through a yawn.

Milos' second-in-command bounded through the door, agitated. "Boss, I think I got something." Roger pointed to a cable news feed on a lofted monitor. A tattered mob had gathered on the snowy steps of some vaguely Balkan looking capital. They chanted slogans and waved banners, but this was no peaceful demonstration. Milos saw desperation in their eyes. He spotted white knuckles squeezing stones and broken bottles – something was about to erupt.

"Is that... Ukraine?"

Roger stumbled with the answer, unsure of how to pronounce the place: "Kyr-gyz-stan."

"Kazakhstan?" Milos raised an eyebrow.

"No, I think it's called Kyrgyzstan."

Milos shrugged. "Get Kaufman."

Several floors below, Milos' one-man think tank was lost in contemplation. Pacing back and forth in mismatched socks, listening to baroque music, Kaufman studied an options valuation model projected on the wall. His slight, angular frame was like an afterthought – a wispy vessel that only existed to bear his brain through space.

Milos kept his secret weapon cloistered in a comfortably appointed office, insulated from the tumult of the killing floor above. Mild-mannered Kaufman decorated it with charts, maps and contemporary paintings. He needed space to think – to tune out the noise and melodrama of constant market gyrations. If Milos knew anything, it was how to read a person – to sniff out what he wanted and what he'd do to get it. Milos paid Kaufman handsomely, but he knew he didn't just work for the money.

The phone rang Kaufman out of his trance.

"Hey... Kyrgyzstan?" Kaufman snickered. "I saw that one coming like a train wreck in slow motion... Sure, I'll be right up."

Still in his socks, Kaufman padded into the maelstrom of traders scrambling for an edge. They were frothier than ever, but Milos and Kaufman shared a cool-headed nod of understanding.

They looked at the monitor and watched the powder keg erupt. Hungry looters smashed store windows, making off with food and clothing. Milos was intimately familiar with the tell-tale facial expressions he read on the screen – the citizens had reached an inflection point. This was the decisive moment when enough of them realized they had nothing left for their leaders to steal. There was no one more dangerous than a man with nothing to lose. A mob of such men could turn the whole country upside down. It was like striking a match – once ignited, there was no turning back. Events would spiral out of control and they wouldn't stop until all of the fuel – the years of abuse, poverty and accumulated resentment – had burned out.

It was an interesting spectacle to witness on a video screen, in a climate-controlled office six thousand miles away. But nothing could be more terrifying to live firsthand.

"They're going to tar the President," Kaufman thought out loud.

"Tar him?!" Roger seemed lost.

"They're going to dip him in tar". Kaufman was only twenty-eight, but his colleagues looked to him like some kind of oracle.

"Seems a little medieval, no?" Milos mused.

"It sends a clear message."

Milos rubbed his hands together in mild excitement. "Okay, what's our angle?"

"I assume you're shorting their currency. I think it's called the Som."

Milos looked over his shoulder, double checking Chaz, his foreign exchange man.

"We're on it." The currency trader pried his stunned eyes up from his screen to force a truckling smile.

"This should also destabilize Kazakhstan's Tenge and the Uzbek Som," Kaufman continued.

"Got that?" Milos saw Chaz clicking furiously at his workstation, playing catch-up.

"Yeah, I'm shorting the hell out of them!" Chaz declared with too much bravado. Chaz had a lamely authoritarian personality – he saw himself on a hierarchical ladder. He obsequiously flattered his superiors and mercilessly condescended to everyone else. All his waking hours were spent trading, weightlifting and chasing whichever women put up the least resistance.

Milos led Kaufman away from the irritating currency man. "What else?"

Kaufman's eyes glazed over as his mind homed in on central Asia. "They export some rare-earth metals... and electricity... but most foreign investment is in agricultural processing."

"How far will this spread?"

"Check the regional exchanges. Energy prices should spike and you can probably expect a nice sell-off on the Kyrgyz Stock Exchange. Poor liquidity should amplify it."

"You with us?" Milos cast a wary eye on his minions, scrambling to harvest the fruits of Kaufman's vision. They nodded excitedly, grunted in the affirmative. The charts on their screens spiked and their trading accounts swelled alongside their egos.

"What's our take?" the patriarch enquired.

"Fifty-three... no sixty-three million," an energy trader declared.

"Twenty-eight on the index," Derrick, an equities trader chimed in. He mentally tallied the effect this win would have on his annual bonus; then translated the sum from dollars to cocaine, sports cars and prostitute-hours.

"Good, cover when it levels out." Milos finally cracked a smile. They had pulled enough loot to get his heart pumping, if only for a moment. "Great work, Kaufman." He turned to gauge the young man's excitement. It registered somewhere south of non-existent.

"You know where to find me." Kaufman turned and ambled back to the mahogany lined elevator. His mind had already returned to the realm of unstructured thought – daydreams, ruminations, creativity. Kaufman spent most of his life drifting in this never-never land. It wasn't the best way to attend to basic survival needs, but it gave birth to innovations and revelations.

"Nice socks," Milos teased.

Kaufman snapped back to earth, looked down and noticed his mismatched feet for the first time. "Oops," he shrugged and retreated to his cloister, leaving his peers bewildered.

2

Bare feet bandied a battered ball, back and forth, across red dirt. The only soccer ball in the village was treasured and abused, torn apart and sewn back together by successive generations of boys, so no one remembered how it got there or who really owned it. It changed custody on occasion, after epic brawls that only ended with the intervention of vexed village elders, threatening to bury the coveted sphere deep in the jungle so it could cause no further trouble.

This Congolese village was so remote and isolated from the outside world that the boys didn't know all the rules of the game, so they made some up to fill in the gaps. The Capital, Kinshasa was so far off it might as well have been in China. Even the nearest neighboring village was a whole day's walk or a few hours away, drifting down the Congo River.

When everything a person did from the cradle to the grave was noticed and remembered, lying and cheating were unheard of. There was little distinction between neighbors and blood relatives.

With no exposure to global culture, people developed strange quirks – their own unique accents and styles of dress. They even walked a little funny. As soon as a girl was born, it was clear to everyone but her, which boy she would wed. It wasn't a result of arranged marriage, but the predictability that came from a limited selection.

The soccer ball wasn't going far, jammed up by a throng of boys, all artlessly kicking at once. They needed a catalyst to break the gridlock. Sebu, the village all-star, sprinted across the dirt and his teammates parted to give him an opening. The opposing team groaned in resignation. His footfalls were precise and measured. He moved without thinking, acting on instinct. Sebu's timing and coordination were perfect. His little foot darted into the center of the fray, tipped the ball up over the opposing boys' heads and before it could touch down on the other side, he was already waiting there to rocket it into the goal – a bushel basket borrowed from the church. His team broke out in a taunting victory dance.

"Very good, Sebu! Now fetch me some water," his lovely mother called out. He pretended not to hear her, savoring his goal and gloating with his friends. A moment later she was in the middle of the mob, pulling Sebu out by his ear. His teammates erupted in laughter. He was always outrunning, outtalking and outthinking them, so they took rare pleasure in seeing him humbled.

Sebu weaved among his neighbors' huts, inhaling the spicy redolence of boiling stews, hearing the mothers singing as they worked, feeling the soft dirt under his feet. He loved his village with all his heart.

Trudging down the narrow trail to the river, he daydreamed and twirled an empty jerry can around his fingers. He crossed paths with his best friend, Lumumba, who lugged a full can homeward.

"Eh, Lumumba! Let's trade cans."

Lumumba looked down at Sebu's empty container and laughed. "No brother, let's trade punches!" They dropped their jerry cans and play-boxed, circling and slapping each other's faces. Tall, gangly Lumumba was well matched against compact, powerful Sebu. Boxing degenerated to wrestling and they collapsed in a laughing, dusty heap in the middle of the trail.

Sebu and Lumumba had been inseparable since they were toddlers, always joking, rough-housing and finding new ways to get into trouble. They played tricks on the girls and constantly competed to impress them.

"We could go fishing," Sebu suggested.

"I wish! Baba needs me to mend a fence," Lumumba groaned.

"Baaaaaah!" Sebu waved him off and slumped onward down the trail.

"Tomorrow, brother. We will catch many fish tomorrow!"

Sebu brightened.

He reached the riverbed and plunged his jerry can into the rushing stream, taking in the rhythmic, lapping water and letting his mind wander. His eyes scanned his surroundings and he noticed they were different than before. Recent flooding had uprooted trees and agitated the muddy bank.

He caught a glint of light reflected in the pebbles, even though they were black. That was odd. He'd never seen stones quite like these before.

Sebu felt a tickle of excitement in his chest. He had heard outlandish tales of other villages striking it rich with oil, gold or diamonds. Perhaps this unfamiliar rock was silver ore. He had been told that his homeland, the Democratic Republic of the Congo, was the most resource-rich country in the world, so anything was possible. Scouts would occasionally visit his village, sniffing out hidden treasure and promising generous remuneration for a strike. So far they had come up empty, so the villagers had to be content to eke out their livelihoods from whatever they could grow, hunt, or make with their hands. Sebu sometimes heard the adults griping that some neighboring village hit pay dirt and a Chinese firm had offered to build them roads and infrastructure in exchange for mineral rights.

Sebu's mother saw him ambling absent-mindedly back to their hut with no jerry can and his eyes fixated on a handful of mud. Halfway through the threshold, he felt a swift crack on his backside from her straw broom.

"Darling boy, where's my water?"

Sebu snapped out of his daydream. "Sorry, Mama."

"If you want me to cook dinner, you better find that can." She waved a threatening finger in Sebu's face. He prayed he hadn't lost it. The family relied on the vessel for drinking and cooking. Even if they had a single franc to their name, no one else in the village had an extra can to sell them.

Sebu slapped the mud on her table and ran off to retrieve the family asset. Mother irritably charged over to clean up after him, when the same glint in the pebbles caught her eye. She, too, felt a tickle in her heart.

That night at dinner, Father stoked the fire of irrational exuberance. He was the village's resident "entrepreneur," always entangled in some ridiculous money making scheme. Most recently, he tried to start a river ferry but found no one had cash for the fare. He ended up shuttling his neighbors back and forth, taking payment in live chickens or cassava stew. His schemes never worked, but everyone admired him for trying. He had enough ambition for the whole village.

"Sebu, you have given a humble father hope! The ore you found can change so much for our family." His baritone boomed through the hut. It was amazing that such a larger-than-life voice came out of such a slight man.

Sebu beamed with pride, but Mother's lips tightened. She had seen her husband get ahead of himself countless times and cleaned up enough of his messes that she couldn't help but feel a little apprehensive.

"Tomorrow I am going with the elders to find an investor to develop our mine!" Father boasted.

"Mine?!" Now even Sebu was overwhelmed. How had father decided that a few glinting, black rocks were reason enough to take on a massive enterprise? Perhaps he wished so intensely to transcend his provincial life, to enjoy the luxuries and novelties he heard about in the city, that he could convince himself of anything.

"Of course – how else will we harvest the metal?" Father chuckled.

"Will the mine be large?" Sebu's demure little sister chimed in. She was the darling of the family – ever graceful and gentle. Sebu would give his life for her.

"Oh yes! People will come from far away to work in our village. We will build a house of bricks! We will not even need our cows anymore."

Sebu looked to Mother in alarm. Now even he sensed Father was drifting past the point of reason.

"Let us not sell our cattle just yet." Mother tried to pull him back to earth, but father was already spending the imminent riches in his mind. He conjured a gold watch on his wrist, a pinstripe suit on his back. Dare he dream of an automobile?

"Woman!" He bellowed. The family leapt a little in their seats. "You must think bigger!"

3

Kaufman slipped out of the imposing lobby, after an uneventful work day. Kyrgyzstan was still in shambles, but the easy cash had already been wrung out of that disaster. There were plenty of other global crises brewing at any given moment, but nothing bubbled over just yet.

The Jupiter Fund would not deign to intercede in any old macroeconomic flare-up. Milos expected massive profit with very low risk. But once the monstrous firm decided to wrap its tentacles around a weakened institution, it would push and pull; squeeze and leverage its immense capital reserves until the prey surrendered or perished. The tentacles slithered all over the world – exerting power, peddling influence, manipulating outcomes in public and private sectors alike. The corporate animal fed on cash and it grew fatter so it could swallow more and more; and it even excreted a little sewage, so people would buzz around like flies, clamoring to do its bidding for a few stray droppings.

But not Kaufman – he averted his eyes from the vulgarity of profit/loss statements. He had built himself an ivory tower atop the hulking beast and studied global economics and interconnectedness with clinical detachment. The Jupiter Fund was the perfect laboratory to test his understanding of how the world worked. Why write dissertations that would only gather dust in academic libraries? Instead he could guide the financial colossus with his mind, trampling through world markets and learning firsthand how people responded to incentives, how fear and greed interplayed in a dance of economic equilibrium.

At the foot of the skyscraper, Kaufman was lost in his thoughts, his earbuds pumping rococo harpsichord trills. He felt a thud against his shoulder that almost knocked him over. Fight or flight kicked in. He yanked out the earbuds and spun in the direction of the hit.

Chaz stood there snickering and Derrick clapped his back with frat boy enthusiasm.

"Hey Kauf, thanks for the tips yesterday!"

"Huh?"

"It was good thinking. It should totally pad our bonuses." Chaz gave him another friendly slug.

"Sure..." Kaufman rubbed his inflamed shoulder.

"Wanna trade commodities?" Derrick broke into a mischievous grin.

Kaufman was bewildered by the question. Had they ever seen him personally trade anything? Was the market even open? "I thought you covered stocks."

"No, he means let's hit the club and pick up some babes." Chaz cracked up laughing and elbowed him in the ribs.

"Ohhhh commodities... yeah, that's funny," Kaufman rolled his eyes. "I can't tonight. I have Pilates."

"The hell you do." They were all going to bond whether he liked it or not.

The sweaty, packed dance floor rocked like Sodom and Gomorrah. Kaufman and his colleagues were lofted in a glass-bottom V.I.P. room overlooking writhing revelers below. Willowy waitresses sold bottles of premium vodka at thousand percent markups to well-heeled hot-shots who happily paid for the privilege of their presence. Traders bumped lines of cocaine from out-of-work models' chests.

Kaufman sat in a corner nursing a scotch, observing the scene like an anthropologist studying simian mating habits. He watched Derrick and Chaz flopping artlessly in the middle of a throng of dancing, nubile bodies. As the night progressed, they ceaselessly swallowed shots of every fermented grain known to man and while their boldness with the ladies soared to embarrassing heights, their coordination and motor skills sunk to abyssal depths.

Something was very wrong with this picture – what did these misguided women really hope to gain from suffering a couple of overcompensated fools? Some free drinks and a fleeting sense of validation? Perhaps a lost weekend of binging on a gaudy sailing vessel?

What qualified a human being to be elevated to the status of "very important person" and granted entry to this luminous chamber? Many of the women were hand-picked by bouncers, from the multitudes of groundlings on the first floor, for exhibiting outward signs of youth and beauty. They were the bait, brought up to lure the whales – the desperate men who were willing to throw reason to the wind and pay five hundred dollars for a fifty dollar bottle of vodka.

A well-manicured hand waved in Kaufman's face. His eyes locked on crimson fingernails, then scanned up the slinky arm to a brunette with high cheekbones and an alpine nose. Her hair was shiny and cut to perfect symmetry, resting on her delicate clavicle.

"What's on your mind?" She coquettishly batted her lashes.

He looked back at her hand. "Why do women paint their fingernails red?"

"I don't know. Do you think it's sexy?"

"I once read that it's meant to resemble blood on your claws. To signal dominance. Like you're a predatory cat."

"*Rrrow*," she growled and pretended to claw at him.

The silly gesture roused something in Kaufman. He felt his blood pumping for the first time in months. The smell of her perfume drifted into his nostrils. Was that lilac?

"Please," he gestured to the chair across from him and she sat. He reached for the bottle in the nearest ice bucket and poured her a glass of champagne. Kaufman noticed the tag sticking up from the back of her designer dress. She probably intended to return it to Bloomingdales after wearing it once. Who was she trying to impress?

"Who are you? Why are you here? What do you want?"

"Whoa," she was flustered, momentarily at a loss for words. Had this brooding guy already seen right through her? She felt like an imposter, trespassing in his rarified world. The doe-eyed girl stood and retreated in shame.

"Wait, please..." He gestured again for her to sit. "That came out wrong. I didn't mean to offend – just to skip the boring pleasantries. I don't understand what any of us are doing here tonight, playing this game, covered in paint and fragrances to disguise the fact that our bodies perspire; lit and made-up to negate the truth that we are all flawed. So when I ask, I really want to know. Who are you?"

"I'm Carrie."

"Kaufman."

Later that night, Carrie puzzled over Kaufman's apartment.

"Does anyone actually live here?"

"I do."

"Do you have another house in Westchester with a wife and kids?" She let out a nervous giggle. "This doesn't look like anyone's home."

"No Carrie, this is my only residence."

"It's so... sterile."

"I work a lot."

"What do you do for fun?"

"More work."

She poked around in astonishment. There wasn't even a television. But there was a Bloomberg terminal spewing an endless stream of data and news.

Kaufman didn't mind her prying. He was observing her, trying to figure her out at the same time. There was something endearing about Carrie once she stopped putting on airs.

"This is really sad." Sincere pity crossed her face.

He failed to fathom her concern. His place was perfectly functional.

"What do you do?" Kaufman changed the subject.

"I don't know. I show up at cattle calls. Sometimes I book a toothpaste ad." She flashed her toilet-bowl white teeth. "I also volunteer at a cat shelter," she added, as if it acquitted her of an otherwise pointless existence.

"And you say I'm sad?" Kaufman cracked a smile. She snickered deprecatingly, nodding to acknowledge his point. They were forming a cheap connection.

"This place needs a woman's touch." She reached out and stroked his stubbly face. Kaufman grabbed her by the waist and they kissed. Then they had awkward sex, without much tenderness — not because they especially liked each other, but because they were drunk and lonely and there wasn't much else to do in his apartment at three in morning.

4

Father and the village elders led their newfound friends to the bank of the river. General Makanga strutted and swaggered, in full military dress uniform with too many medals dangling from his chest. No man could have earned them all – perhaps he ordered them from eBay. But father and the elders didn't know better, so they were duly impressed. Makanga was a colossal figure – his every physical feature exaggerated like a caricature of a manly man. His meaty hands could crush bones. His massive teeth could chew through rope. The general was accompanied by a skinny, skittish geologist in thick glasses and a ratty brown suit.

"The river is speckled with silver ore," Father announced, making a grandiose gesture at the muddy riverbed. The elders smiled at his expert salesmanship – he would surely negotiate a favorable price.

With trembling fingers, the geologist gingerly removed a test tube from his lapel pocket and bent down to scoop a soil sample. He held it up to his face and squinted, scrutinizing the stones.

Father and the elders wondered why the man was so nervous. Was he having a bad day? Makanga seemed perfectly content – like the cat that swallowed the canary.

"This is not silver," the geologist sheepishly whispered.

The villagers deflated. Makanga's smug smile disappeared and his face turned chillingly sinister. The elders' hearts were seized with a dark premonition.

"Don't bluff me to get a better price!" Father blustered, trying to conceal his chagrin.

"It's coltan," the geologist continued, immediately wincing.

"Coltan?" The elders repeated in confusion.

"Even better!" Makanga announced.

What a foolish bargaining tactic, Father thought. Why would
the general admit his desire for this mysterious substance? Father
would surely get the best of this amateur. "Great – let us negotiate!"

"Yes..." Makanga smiled menacingly.

Father didn't pick up on it. "We have a list..."

Makanga drew his pearl handled .45 sidearm and blasted Father
in the torso. The hollow point round battered through his sternum,
mushroomed and splintered in his chest cavity, tearing his heart to
shreds. His eyes were frozen in shock as he died on his feet. The elders
shrieked and ran, but Makanga shot them both in the back. The last
thing they saw was their viscera erupting from their chests.

The geologist shuddered as blood spattered on his glasses.
Makanga holstered his weapon and basked in the ecstasy of predation.

The village buzzed with excitement. Speculation ran rampant –
what glorious windfall was in store for them? Would the children
get a new soccer ball? Might the elders fix the leaky roof of the
church? Was it absurd to wish for a television with a satellite dish?

Sebu and his enterprising father had been heaped with praise and
gratitude. No longer would their village be second-rate. Sebu's discovery stood to fast-track them all into the modern world. The family
modestly declined a shower of fruits and gifts from their neighbors.

Outside Sebu's hut was a bubbling cauldron of nervous,
hopeful anticipation. Sister helped Mother cook, while Sebu alternated between pestering them and peering into the distance
for Father's return. He couldn't contain himself – his whole body
trembled with excitement.

"Where will all the workers live?" Sebu needled his mother. She threw her palms up, exasperated from days of unrelenting questions. Was she the only one who smelled trouble?

"I do not know," she groaned.

"Could I have a bicycle? I always wanted a bicycle!" Sebu pulled at her sleeve.

"I do not know," she chanted again, like a mantra.

"I want a new dress!" Sister finished shucking corn and threw the last ear down with finality, as if she'd never have to sully her hands with manual labor again.

"You may have seven new dresses," Sebu proclaimed, suddenly feeling magnanimous.

"Thank you!" She beamed with gratitude and tackled Sebu with a hug.

"Children!" They startled. "I do not completely understand the situation. So let us save our excitement for later."

They finally realized how nervous Mother was, so they took deep breaths and feigned calm, dutifully returning to their chores. Their exaggerated seriousness lasted for about half a minute before they broke into another round of teasing and laughter.

A villager ambled by carrying fish and whistling a happy tune. His head burst open like an overripe tomato and his body gave out from under him, collapsing in an inanimate heap in the dirt. The report echoed through the village a fraction of a second later.

Sebu froze in shock. One second that man was alive, about to enjoy a feast of fish with his family, the next second he was a corpse. His memories and personality took years to develop, but an instant to erase. What was happening? Sebu strained to process it, but his mind was stuck.

The village erupted in screaming pandemonium, everyone scrambling for dear life. Sebu did not know how to react. His neighbors had always comported themselves with dignity and grace, rarely raising their voices in anger, and now they were screeching and flailing around like desperate, cornered animals.

Automatic weapons opened fire from every direction. There was nowhere to run. The villagers were completely encircled by unseen killers.

"Get inside!" Mother barked, shoving her children into the hut. Sebu drifted along with her, but he didn't feel much – like he was just floating through a confusing dream.

She pushed their heads down to the floor and darted furtive glances out the window. Mother looked on in horror as grim-faced mercenaries charged out of the jungle, AK-47 assault rifles spraying bullets indiscriminately at men, women and children alike. Sebu's friends and neighbors were torn apart, slaughtered like livestock.

Several villagers ran to the church for refuge and barricaded themselves behind heavy wooden doors. A rocket propelled grenade screamed low across the sky and blew the church to splinters, charring most inside. A couple survivors leapt out of the debris, still on fire and were gunned down.

The mercenaries torched huts and dragged young girls, kicking and screaming, into the jungle to satisfy their beastly urges.

Mother and sister broke out into hysterics, while Sebu was still paralyzed with fear.

"Where is Father?" Sister demanded.

They felt a rush of heat and looked up to see their roof ablaze.

Mother forced herself to focus. She grabbed her children's faces to drill in her point. "We must run into the jungle. It is our only hope. If anything happens to me, you must keep running."

"Why are we being attacked?" Sebu's eyes were glassy and dilated. He almost sounded calm, but he was really just in shock. Mother slapped him hard across the face to bring him back to her. He shook his head and snapped out of his daze. The sounds of screaming and gunfire outside now felt immediate. Sebu's mind shifted to animal instinct, fight or flight.

"I don't know. Just promise whatever happens you will run as fast as you can," Mother screamed in their faces.

The children nodded meekly.

Sebu and his family burst out of their hut and ran for dear life.

Mother was immediately shot. The round punched through her chest and knocked her on her back. She hemorrhaged blood. The children crouched to her aid. The bullet had missed her vital organs. Sebu pressed the wound and tried to stanch the flow, but it was no use.

"I said go!" She sputtered, her tongue awash with blood. She shoved them toward the jungle with her last ounce of strength. They reluctantly ran.

But Sister turned back to tend to Mother. Sebu pulled her off.

"We promised," he implored. She grudgingly followed him.

"I love you," Mother gasped, before another shot silenced her.

Teary-eyed Sebu and his sister reached the outskirts of the village, mere paces from the relative safety of the jungle.

Makanga emerged from the foliage, strolling in late for the slaughter, standing directly in their path. They stopped dead in their tracks. Makanga looked Sister up and down, whistled lecherously though his teeth.

The children looked up in horror, at the colossus looming over them like a nightmare. He blotted out the sun. They tried to dodge around him, but he swatted them both to the dirt with the back of his ogreish hand.

"What a lovely gift!" Makanga slung Sister over his shoulder. She wriggled and screamed. Sebu saw red. He charged at Makanga, his fear dampened by rage. The general drew his pistol and blasted Sebu in the shoulder, missing his heart but knocking him flat on the earth. Makanga tossed writhing Sister like rag doll, into the nearest hut, then charged in after her.

Sebu strained to stand and save her, but his world went black.

5

Hung over in his kitchenette, Kaufman crunched Cocoa Puffs and vegetated in front of his Bloomberg terminal. Chewing sent dull, stabbing pains into his head, so he decided to stick to orange juice. Carrie held dominion over his bed, sprawled out across its width, groaning through an even mightier headache.

Kaufman watched a clueless finance reporter drone on about the unintended consequences of the Jupiter Fund's geopolitical meddling:

"...Deposed Kyrgyz President Bystrovka held a press conference in Moscow, since he was exiled from his homeland..."

The video feed cut to a dilapidated hotel conference room with peeling wallpaper. A disheveled Slavic politician ranted at a rickety podium, manically gesticulating, showering the microphones with spit. He appeared to be scratching the remnants of tar from his skin. His ill-fitting suit made him look like a used car salesman. Bystrovka's native language was muted and a translator's voice dubbed over:

"...why should my people suffer because some profiteering Wall Street Jews wish to crush our small economy; to feed their bloated bellies with the sweat and blood of our poor workers? Take me back, my people. Take me into your hearts and I will close our companies off from foreign investment and shield our citizens from the predatory evil of the Milos Sterlings of this world..."

"Jackass," Kaufman muttered under his breath, as he stood to wash out his cereal bowl. He checked on Carrie and found her snoring, her eye makeup smeared like a raccoon and a widening circle of drool on her pillow. He left her to convalesce on his bed.

He was already out the door and didn't hear the reporter continue:

"...The former president was of course referring to the ninth richest man, Milos Sterling, whose Jupiter Fund led the stampede of global divestment from Kyrgyzstan's economy, resulting in the crash which many fear will lead to a national depression. Mr. Sterling was not available for comment."

Jogging on a treadmill, Milos watched the same report with equal ennui. He paid as much attention to his other screens, which played a documentary about ancient Mesopotamia and an auction of post-impressionist watercolors, respectively.

Milos stepped off the treadmill and his chef was already waiting with a foul wheatgrass concoction, while his trainer stretched in preparation for their morning regimen of Greco-Roman grappling.

Kaufman's path to work was blocked by a news crew. He found himself surrounded by cameras, with a microphone shoved in his face. They all shouted questions at once, their volume hammering at his hungover ears.

"Sir, do you work for the Jupiter Fund?" a combative reporter demanded to know.

Kaufman grunted a weak affirmative and ducked around them. He was halfway in the revolving door, when the pushy journo called out:

"Do you feel your firm is responsible for Kyrgyzstan's economic collapse?"

A twinge of irritation shot through his aching brain and he decided not to let it go. He spun back around and faced the news crew down.

"Have you been listening to that crook, Bystrovka? He's a desperate man. He's grasping for a scapegoat, but he won't find one in us. It may be convenient to blame foreign financiers for his nation's collapse, but he should really blame himself. If his own people cannot trust him, how can we? When he lies about his capital reserves, when he knowingly cooks his economic data, when he steals from taxpayers and appoints thieves to high office, how can we feel safe investing in him? His credit is bad and we treated him accordingly. Sure, we made money from his failure – but we could as easily have profited from his success."

Kaufman regained his composure and marched back in, leaving grateful reporters with some juicy sound bites.

After work, Kaufman paid his weekly penance at the Garcia Youth Center in the Bronx. The walls were covered in graffiti and the building smelled like an unwashed sock. Underprivileged pre-teens ran him ragged on the scuffed basketball court. They showed off, passed the ball through his legs and took every opportunity to taunt and ridicule his athletic ineptitude.

Juan made a three-pointer through Kaufman's outstretched arms. It sunk straight through the warped hoop, despite a missing backboard.

"You lose, Kaufman!" The mohawked twelve-year-old broke into a wobbly-kneed victory dance he learned from a rap video.

"You win..." Kaufman panted, "...a math lesson!" The children groaned.

In a crumbling classroom, under flickering fluorescent lights, Kaufman failed to rein them in. He pointed to a simple algebra problem on the chalkboard: $5X = 10$.

"Who can solve for X?"

Some kids stared blankly. Most talked and played amongst themselves.

"Anyone?"

"X is just a letter, homie!" Juan looked puzzled.

"Right, but it represents a number in the equation. Five times that unknown number, equals ten. Can you figure out what the number is?"

"We haven't learned this stuff yet," Juan protested. The other kids backed him up with raucous pleas to change the subject.

Kaufman sighed. He spotted Tito and Leon playing craps in the back. A mischievous grin crossed his face. They were so involved in their game that they didn't notice him creep forward and hover over them. He silently watched them play for a moment and the rest of the class fell silent as well, eagerly awaiting the outcome. Would he yell or kick them out? They hoped for some entertaining wrath.

The scrappy little troublemakers finally looked up and saw Kaufman leaning over them. They winced, bracing themselves for punishment.

"Craps?" Kaufman looked bemused. They nodded guiltily. "What are you rolling for?"

"Five," Leon mumbled sheepishly, still steeling himself for Kaufman's rage. Couldn't he just get it over with? The suspense was painful.

"Do you know what your chances are?"

Leon shook his head. Was he actually not in trouble? The class broke out in confused murmurs.

"If you want to make some money, you better know the probability!" Kaufman picked up the dice, returned to the chalkboard and started diagramming outcomes. Now the children paid close attention.

6

Sebu's eyelids opened to slits, too swollen to spread any wider. All he could see was a blur of light and color. His head felt empty and buoyant, as if it hovered over him like a balloon; while his body was weighed down with pain.

He squeezed his eyes shut again and prayed that it was all just a nightmare, that he was merely sick with a fever and his mind was playing tricks on him. He smelled cooking meat and imagined he was in his soft bed and Mother was treating him to a stew. He would rise and share breakfast with his loving family. Sebu forced his eyes open and saw scorched corpses all around, with expressions of terror seared on their faces.

He jolted upright, but his shoulder screamed and throbbed. The pain anchored him to the ground. He strained his neck and saw the bullet entry wound was scabbed over. How long was he out? He twisted his head past excruciation to see the back of his shoulder. The exit wound was gaping, mangled and caked with mud – which probably saved him from bleeding to death.

With gritted teeth and agony, he rolled onto his good side to see vultures picking the eyes from bodies strewn about the charred huts. Deeper in the distance, a pair of straggling mercenaries scavenged the apocalyptic ruins of the village, frisking the dead and sifting through rubble for valuables.

A mercenary looked in Sebu's direction. The boy froze, trying to make his eyes look lifeless. The soldier squinted, tilted his head in contemplation and slowly crept over, his assault rifle dangling casually at his side. Sebu's heart raced, but he forced himself to take shallow, imperceptible breaths. If the mercenary got too close, he couldn't take the risk of breathing at all.

And soon the monster loomed right over him. Sebu prayed the man would be convinced of his death and wander off before Sebu's body would involuntarily heave and gasp for air.

The mercenary jabbed Sebu's stomach with the tip of his weapon, but Sebu made no sound. He knelt down and rummaged through Sebu's pockets. Sebu stayed limp and hoped the mercenary would not hear the machine-gun pounding of his heart.

He caught a fleeting a glimpse of the man's battle-scarred face and toothless maw. He inhaled the slightest whiff and was overwhelmed by acrid body odor and boozy breath.

"These people have nothing!" The mercenary called out to his friend, then sauntered back, satisfied that Sebu was both dead and destitute.

Sebu sucked air as silently as he could, waited until the war mongers were distracted, then slithered on his belly to the cover of the jungle. He tried to compress himself so flat against the ground that he ate dirt along the way.

Sebu feared he'd be spotted and shot before he could make it to safety. Would he even feel the slug that killed him, or would his head just explode in a mist of blood and bone, like that man carrying fish? At least his neighbor died happy – instantly shut down before he knew his whole world was ending.

The setting sun splattered across the sky like a fried egg and Sebu kept running deeper and deeper into the unknown, fueled by adrenaline and primal fear. He had no sense of time or location.

He was just trying to get himself away from that hellish place. Everyone he loved was dead and everything he thought he knew about the world was wrong.

Sebu hadn't sensed his eyes acclimating to diminishing light, but now the sun was gone and they had nothing left to work with. Even the moon was obscured by a canopy of trees. He was immersed in darkness, with no food, tattered clothes and no clue where he was.

Animals howled in the distance. He wondered if he'd make it through the night.

Exhaustion finally hit him like an avalanche. He had burned every ounce of energy he had, to get himself to this point and now he felt his body giving up. He knew he needed rest, but without some kind of shelter from those distant beasts, they would smell his fresh blood and make a meal of him.

Sebu found a sturdy tree and achingly climbed it. His shoulder throbbed, so he used his bad side for balance while his good limbs did the heavy lifting. He reached a thick, low branch and wedged his body so he could sleep without falling out and breaking his neck. He tore off part of his shirt to improvise a bandage.

Sebu could hold his feelings in no longer. Throughout the devastating ordeal, he had to muzzle himself for survival. Now that he had a quiet moment alone, Sebu broke down and cried himself to sleep like the child that he was.

He was jolted frequently from his nightmares, by bouts of vertigo and the chill of the howling wind.

Voices approached and Sebu awoke in a panic. It was now broad daylight. How long had he slept? Could the mercenaries have caught up with him? Maybe he had run around in circles and never made it far from home. The voices grew louder and they sounded bitter and dangerous. Sebu tried to hide his body behind a branch, but it would not fit. He heard their clomping footfalls grow louder and he held his breath again, pleading with God that he would not be spotted and shot down from the tree.

A rush of relief washed over him, when tattered refugees emerged from the brush. They carried rusty, makeshift weapons that were just as damaged as they were – a bent spear, a dull machete. He knew they posed no threat to him, because he had nothing of value to take.

"Excuse me," he called down in a meek voice. Even that made the trekkers leap out of their skin, since they too had their world torn out from under them.

Gripping their crude implements, the broken people shot up a panicked look. Then they let out a collective sigh of relief when they saw a scared little boy quivering on a branch, rather than another platoon of killers waiting in ambush.

"What are you doing up there, boy?" Their elder called up, as amused as a devastated man could be. His face was weathered like an ancient desert.

"My village was destroyed," Sebu murmured.

"Ours as well. Come with us."

He tremblingly inched down the tree, scraping his skin against the bark.

Sebu trudged along with them, slouching and defeated. But he took a little comfort in sharing the journey with someone.

"General Makanga is taking all the land in our region. I wish there were nothing of value in the earth. Then we would be left alone," the elder explained.

"Where are we going?" Sebu enquired.

"Across the border. We will be safe there."

"How far is it?"

"I do not know."

That was a good enough answer for now. It seemed like a better plan than dying alone.

That night, Sebu gathered with his temporary family around a fire, restoring in him the slightest shred of normalcy. The smell of burning still unsettled him, but at least they had no meat to eat. The aroma of cooking flesh would surely crack his floodgates of emotion. He had enough difficulty forcing back raw memories.

A woman breastfed her infant. A young man pounded his fists in frustration. An elder woman doled out small, boiled cassava roots — one per person. Sebu scarfed his ration.

"Chew slowly. You may not eat again soon," warned the elder man. But it was too late. He had practically inhaled the meager morsel. The elder man sighed. He reached to check under Sebu's wound dressing. "It is infected."

After much protestation, Sebu submitted to the elders' wisdom. Two of the stronger refugees held him down as he screamed and writhed in pain. The elder woman used a pair of sharpened twigs to dig out leftover fragments of the .45 caliber slug, plunking them one by one into a tin cup.

Sebu had never felt such agony in his life, but by now he was growing numb to pain.

The elder woman sewed him shut as the elder man smeared on a medicinal paste he had extracted from the surrounding trees.

The motley band of survivors hobbled onward at sunrise. They were weaker and hungrier than ever. Their rations barely held them over for an hour. Cassava root was pure starch and empty calories, with virtually no nutritional content. Their vacuous stomachs screamed and pleaded for more, but they knew they had to at least try to make their supply last.

Sebu's eyes were glassy and delirious with fever. The infection had spread all over his body. He stumbled down the path, unable to walk straight, foggy headed and dizzy. He barely remembered who he was.

The refugees heard voices in the nearby brush. The panicked elder threw up a hand signal and everyone halted dead in their tracks. The voices grew louder and closer. They all huddled together in hopes of avoiding detection, their sweat and fear puddling on the ground beneath them. But Sebu was oblivious. His mind was elsewhere – playing soccer and embracing his family in the clouds.

Branches parted and another band of refugees emerged from a converging trail. Hearts on both sides leapt – first with fear, then with joy at the sight of kindred spirits. The new exiles looked equally tattered and broken. They were led by an even older elder, with a face that was pockmarked like the moon. The elders met in the middle.

"Welcome." Sebu's elder extended his arms.

"Welcome to what, brother?" The older man enquired.

"Welcome to dirt!" The elders laughed wistfully and embraced.

The rest of the refugees greeted each other and pressed the flesh. Sebu was too dazed to exchange pleasantries. And soon they were all trudging the trail again.

A lanky boy in the back caught a glimpse of Sebu and shoved through the line to greet him.

"You're alive!" Lumumba exclaimed, literally jumping for joy. Sebu couldn't hear through his delirium. "Sebu?" Lumumba's throat tightened. Was this shell-shocked boy just a mirage of Lumumba's wishful thinking? Or was his best friend angry at him? Why didn't he answer?

Sebu kept slogging forward like a zombie. All the commotion around him felt like a distant murmur, like a faded memory.

"Sebu!" Lumumba shouted. "I thought you were gone forever." Sebu swatted Lumumba away, not registering who he was or what he was saying – only that someone was loud and irritating in his face.

Lumumba's heart sank. He boxed Sebu's ear in frustration. A painful ringing snapped Sebu out of his daze. He spun angrily, then finally saw his faithful friend. Sebu embraced Lumumba with shaky arms. Both boys burst into tears, which were quickly stifled – stoicism deeply ingrained in their upbringing.

"I thought we were all dead." Sebu's voice was barely a whisper.

"Don't worry, there is still time for that."

Sebu mustered a meek laugh. He squeezed Lumumba to make sure he was really there. "Were there any other survivors?" He did not allow hope to creep into his voice.

Lumumba hung his head. They continued walking close together in silence.

7

Holed up in his office, Kaufman was mesmerized by his monitors. There had been some bizarre behavior in the markets, but he couldn't quite place it. Oil prices had entirely decoupled from the realities of supply and demand, barreling skyward for no reason at all. He rang one of his counterparts at an Indian firm, an old friend from MIT.

"Sujeet, it doesn't add up. If Venezuela, Canada and Norway average 3 million barrels a day..."

"Round-trip trades," Sujeet cut him off. Kaufman got the drift – prices were manipulated by big players, selling and instantly buying back oil contracts at progressively higher prices, artificially driving up the market.

"They're pulling that again? It's gonna blow up in their faces."

"I doubt it. These guys are slippery."

Kaufman rolled his eyes. He wouldn't have been shocked if the whole scheme had been born a few floors above. He kept stumbling on new variations of the same old tricks. There was no corner of the market free of monkey business – nothing new under the sun. Was the job starting to bore him?

Milos peeked into the office. Kaufman blinked in disbelief. Had Sterling ever even set foot on this floor? Was Kaufman in some sort of trouble?

"Kaufman," Milos whispered, cagey and discreet.

"Gotta go." He hastily hung up on Sujeet.

"You are fluent in French?" Milos raised a bushy eyebrow.

"More or less," Kaufman hesitated. He wasn't bad at Mandarin, Russian or Portuguese either, but he had no idea why his boss wanted to know.

"You are not busy Saturday?"

"Uh, not particularly." There was only one right answer.

"I need to discuss something important and private. Please come to my Westchester home. You know how to get there?"

Kaufman nodded. He had made his obligatory appearances at the annual "Vulture's Feast" – a vulgar, showy affair for which Milos gathered clients and competitors alike, to gloat about the year's returns and buy their admiration with rare delicacies and pompous spectacles. It was rather tasteless, for a man with such impeccable taste.

"Nine A.M. And don't mention it to anyone."

"Right."

Milos smiled slightly and walked out. Kaufman felt queasy. He knew that look – the old svengali was up to something. Sterling could be a cipher at times, entirely opaque and imperceptible. Sometimes his machinations were not even clear to his closest friends.

Would Kaufman be dragged into some outlandish plot? He had always been averse to risk and careful to keep his hands spotless, but Milos was a gambler at heart. Kaufman's mind raced through countless scenarios and speculations, but only time would tell.

8

The jungle had thinned and the pack of refugees now slogged through scrubby, deforested land. The parched earth was hard and scratchy under their blistered feet. Their numbers had swelled, with more desperate, displaced people joining the death march every day. So many faces were fixed in the same blank, hopeless stare. They had all grown sicker and skinnier, bickering over whatever scraps they could scrape along the way. Vultures circled overhead. The trail was littered with corpses, but even the living were starting to decay. Their weakened bodies were afflicted with plagues and pestilence.

Whenever they came across an intact village, they would plod through some variation of the same sad routine:

The villagers would see the vanguard of the ranks, advancing from a distance. Their upbringing dictated that the needy should be welcomed with open arms. But once the refugees brought the scent of death upon the village, the locals thought twice about their charity. By then it was too late. The elders urged their people to prepare food and medicine to care for their fellow human beings. They scrambled to the exiles' aid, amazed that anyone could have made it so far in such a squalid state.

But there would be no end to the flow of sick and hungry travelers. As the village was swarmed, the panicked elders realized their mistake. They had to compromise their values for their own survival. They marshaled their people to cast the refugees out, sometimes at the tip of their spears. No village could sustain such a vast horde of starving humanity, descending on it like a plague of locusts. As they watched the refugees hobble off into the distance, they were gripped with guilt – knowing that the exiles would likely die. And a little part of the villagers died with them.

But those same familiar faces would eventually appear at the end of the line, once Makanga's mercenaries had swallowed their homes as well. Fueled by money from the coltan in Sebu's village, Makanga's forces spread across the land like a cancer, devouring all the natural resources along the way.

Sebu had atrophied to a dry husk of what he used to be. His withered body hobbled down the trail, skeletal legs dragging in the dust, his brain boiled down to its most primitive core. He wasn't near death – he had somehow passed it, shuffling onward like a headless chicken.

"We are almost there," his elder announced in a weak whisper, if only to convince himself.

"He has been saying that for days," Sebu croaked into Lumumba's ear. He took another step, then his legs gave out from under him and he collapsed. Lumumba tried to pull him up with what little strength he had left, but he couldn't get him off the ground.

"I'll just take a little rest." Sebu rolled out of the way of lumbering feet, to lie under a barren tree. The naked, knotty branches looked as sick as his limbs. Refugees kept shuffling past, too weak to care. The vultures swooped into a tight holding pattern overhead, sensing the imminence of their next meal. Sebu's vision went blurry and his eyes slowly closed.

"Get up!" Lumumba screamed, straining his parched throat.

"No." Sebu attempted to wave him away, but could barely lift his arm.

"Everyone is walking. We are almost there," Lumumba pleaded.

"A little sleep."

"Are you stupid? No one who falls asleep on this trail ever wakes up."

"It's fine. I'll see you soon." Sebu slipped deeper into oblivion.

"I've lost everything. I can't lose you here."

"I'm so hungry. Just let me sleep."

Lumumba slapped Sebu hard across the face. Sebu's eyes widened. They focused for the first time in days – locking on Lumumba. Feeble embers still burned within his gaze.

"Get up! Now! If you sleep you will die! We are going *now*." Lumumba strained to lift Sebu to his feet. Sebu dug deep within himself and found the strength to rise, if only for the love of his friend. They hobbled onward to catch up with their group.

The vultures broke formation in search of new opportunities, of which there was no shortage.

9

Kaufman took the train upstate out of Grand Central. His knee bounced nervously as lush greenery zoomed by the window. He had never been alone with Milos and barely saw him outside the office. What did the man want and why was it so private? Milos was not one to be denied anything from his subjects. Whatever he asked of them was granted without hesitation.

Kaufman never admitted it, but Milos Sterling made him feel uneasy. It wasn't that he was afraid for his job – given his talents, it was clearly not at stake. But Kaufman couldn't quite wrap his mind around his boss. He showed different faces to different people. Kaufman had seen quite a few of them over the years, but he had yet to meet the real Milos Sterling. Working for the Jupiter Fund meant wading into moral ambiguity, but how deep was he willing to go?

A lot of people on Wall Street had a 'tough guy' image, but Sterling was legit. He had emerged as the last man standing in plenty of street fights and had been down his share of dark alleys with no name. Milos was well connected in intelligence circles.

Kaufman took a cab to the outskirts of Sterling Manor, a monstrous estate modeled after the palace at Versailles. Expecting his arrival, an Israeli security officer waved him through the screening checkpoint. Kaufman trekked up the expansive lawn, past topiary gardens and classical sculptures, under observation of panning surveillance cameras.

A ramrod-rigid butler led Kaufman past 17th century furniture and paintings worth more than the gross domestic product of Belize. Kaufman wondered who Milos was trying to impress.

They reached the vineyard in the back and Kaufman was seated across from an uncharacteristically casual Milos, barefoot in chinos and a polo shirt. The air was fresh and fragrant with the smell of ripe grapes. Instead of the urban clamor that Kaufman had grown so accustomed to, the only sounds he heard were birds chirping and the vines gently swaying in the breeze.

"Something to drink?"

"I'm fine."

"Bring us an eighty-nine Petrus," Milos commanded the butler, who discreetly raised an eyebrow. He knew this vintage was reserved for special occasions.

"Promise me one thing," Milos leaned in and whispered near Kaufman's ear, his teeth bared either in a smile or a snarl – it was yet unclear.

"Sure," Kaufman's palms were already soaked.

"Whatever happens, do not mention this discussion to anyone." It was definitely more of a snarl.

"Of course." Kaufman felt himself being drawn into some kind of Watergate.

"What do you know about The Democratic Republic of the Congo?" Milos asked.

"It's a bloody, ungovernable mess."

"Sure, but it's the most resource-rich mess in the world." He produced a mineral map of central Africa and pointed to the D.R.C., with its bountiful deposits. Kaufman knew he wasn't there for a geology lesson. And nothing good ever happened in the Congo. Something ugly was about to bubble to the surface. "Diamonds, copper, oil, gold, zinc, uranium, coltan…" Milos shot Kaufman a coy look, "You know about coltan?"

"It's used to make capacitors. It's in almost every electronic device ever sold."

"There's a growth industry," Milos snickered.

"I hear when Sony releases a new Playstation, the price of coltan spikes like crazy."

"Right. It just so happens there is a very rich coltan operation available in the Congo."

"Available?" Kaufman sighed. Available could mean many different things in central Africa – available to buy; available to steal; available to coerce or bribe a sweetheart deal from a vulnerable, high ranking government official whose salary was lower than that of an American working part-time at McDonalds.

Kaufman should have seen this coming. Milos had been scouring the world for mineral rights, so he could sit back and suck wealth out of the earth, like a Saudi king. And while the era of fossil fuels was coming to an end, the digital age was just beginning. There was limited coltan on the planet – most of it in the Congo. The demand for semiconductors kept growing with every successive generation of new technology. If Milos could just get a footing, the wily fox could turn a toehold into a stranglehold. And then he could set whatever price he wanted. It would be a monopoly like DeBeers, but with a product people actually needed. He'd have the world by the balls.

"One General Makanga is looking for project financing."

"General or Warlord?" Kaufman wanted to make it clear from the start, that he wasn't drinking the Kool-Aid on this one. Even if he went along with the plan, he wasn't going to buy the hype.

"You know the drill," Milos conceded.

"How long can he keep it?"

"Not long. Unless he gets strong international backing. He needs stability, legitimacy and development funds. We can provide all these things."

"In exchange for?"

"A controlling interest." That was the proverbial dangling carrot that was juicy enough for Milos Sterling to stick his neck out.

Kaufman felt the way the wind was blowing. He could sense Milos had made up his mind, so he had better at least pay the prospect lip service. "You want me to run the numbers?"

Milos shook his head.

"Should I look over their business plan?"

"I need you to visit."

Kaufman choked and spit out over a thousand dollars worth of wine. "Sir, that isn't really my..."

"Kaufman, I know you don't like to get your hands dirty. But you're the best analyst I have and the only one I can trust with this sort of thing. You're the only one with the perspective to grasp the big picture. You know the other boys – they're not as sharp. They'll be blinded by greed. I need your eyes on this."

"You want me to fly to central Africa?!" Kaufman stammered. He was caught so far off-guard he wasn't living up to his razor-sharp reputation. His heart rate quickened and his breathing grew labored. Milos noticed and tried to placate him.

"Just assess the situation. Does it seem stable *enough*? Is the management rational? Will they be relatively transparent? Gather some data. Hear their offer. Maybe bring us back a soil sample." He spoke in soothing tones.

"This can't be safe..." Kaufman felt waves of nausea. He had read the state department reports on the region. The government had no control over vast expanses of jungle that were overrun by countless, warring rebel factions. There was no rule of law. Outsiders did not set foot in the place without a very good reason. Kaufman would stick out like a golden opportunity.

"The general promises to guard you with his life."

"I'm sure you know someone more qualified." Kaufman knew such promises weren't worth a speck of dust.

"I want to keep this in the family. Everything must remain secret. No one can know you're there — not the media, not the U.N. Don't discuss who sent you. The political situation, the mine, nothing can be leaked — or we will lose our privileged offer. They want to announce all the changes once they've secured strong backing. You realize how fast the Chinese would jump on this deal? I paid dearly for the inside track."

Kaufman stammered "I have to..."

"...Think about it?" Milos interrupted. He was losing patience — he had grown accustomed to blind faith from his employees. Perhaps that's why he valued Kaufman's opinion so much. "Listen Kaufman, this is good for everyone. We can make billions and we can be a stabilizing force in the region."

Kaufman clearly wasn't convinced.

"If this goes through, I'll make you an equity partner in the mine. You know what kind of fuck-you money that translates to?"

Kaufman knew all too well. But every yacht, jet and private island in the world wouldn't mean much to a dead man.

10

The land was now barren. Everyone and everything for miles was either dead or dying. Neither sprout nor sapling emerged from the scorched terrain. The line of refugees had thinned, as their limbs had withered and their bodies consumed themselves to keep their weak hearts sputtering.

Somehow Sebu and Lumumba were still on their feet, albeit barely, leaning hard on each other as they limped down the path – their brains fried, without a coherent thought between the two of them.

Their compatriots dropped like flies all around them, collapsing mid-step; but by now the boys couldn't afford the energy to turn their heads to look. Sacks of skin and bones made soft thuds as they fell to the ground. Emaciated frames caused little impact against the dirt. The dead were set free from all-consuming torment.

The stench of rotting, unwashed people followed the train of exiles like a toxic cloud. They would secrete so much water, salt and minerals from their bodies, under the relentlessly beating sun, to the point that their skin became tough and leathery like cured meat. The fluid would dry on their skin as they shivered through the night. Then they would break a fresh sweat on the next day's slog. Layer upon layer of bacterial putrescence would coat their skin and by the time they fell dead, they already smelled like they had been decomposing for weeks.

Sebu's dry, bloodshot eyes squinted in the distance. He saw a monstrous formation of barbed wire, slung low across the horizon, wider and deeper than he could fathom, enclosing a mass of tents and people so far away they looked like little brown specks. But he could read their body language and they were all bent and broken.

"Is that a prison?" Sebu wondered if this was the reward for which they had tortured and decimated their bodies and souls.

"We are saved!" A man creaked, loud and gravely.

The half-dead refugees broke into a zombie stampede — limping, hobbling, straining to reach salvation, kicking up clouds of dust, choking and coughing all the way to the electrified razor-wire.

Sebu and Lumumba were squeezed through the bottleneck of the entry gate, their flimsy bodies flailing through like discarded trash.

They joined a line — not knowing what exactly for, but because everyone else was doing it. Sebu had a moment to catch his breath and take in the enormity of the camp. What was this mass of mangled humanity doing on so much sterile, useless land? How could they ever feed themselves? Where could they aspire to go after this? Sebu realized he had hit a dead-end.

At least they were given water bottles in line. Sebu and Lumumba guzzled their rations and felt the fluid coursing through their dried up veins. And while it felt so good for the few seconds that they desperately sucked down water, it wasn't nearly enough to make up the deficit. Given a taste of plenty, their bodies cried out and begged for more.

Once they reached the front of the line, the boys were accosted by an overeager aid worker. Chirping through a put-on smile, she said: "This is your ration card — you use it to get food from the distribution center." The well-meaning volunteer pointed to the largest tent, with a line of stick-figure refugees stretching as far as the eye could see.

Sebu and Lumumba didn't entirely hear her. They were mesmerized by the blinding whiteness of her skin. They had never seen such a person before. Her hair was yellow like corn and her eyes were blue like the sky. She had a strong smell of cocoa-butter, from the gallons of sunscreen she had to religiously slather on to avoid frying.

"Does she have a disease?" Lumumba whispered.

"She looks like a ghost," Sebu mused.

They took a couple steps in the direction of the food tent, when Sebu collapsed in an exhausted heap.

He was torn from a dream of idyllic family life, by the sound of desperate groans. Where was he? How long was he out? He strained himself upright, and peered around to see wailing patients, bleeding through their bandages. A one-legged man practiced hobbling with an improvised prosthetic – his stump sat in half of a two-liter soda bottle affixed to the end of a sawed-off crutch.

Sebu realized he was deep in an overcrowded medical tent. The sharp odor of antiseptic wrestled with the festering stench of infection. He would have been horrified, but he had already seen much worse.

He looked down and found an I.V. needle lodged in his arm. He yanked it out in a panic. A Zambian nurse rushed over and wrestled him to plunge it back in.

"No young man, you are still severely dehydrated!"

He eventually relented and let her re-stick him. "Where am I? Where is Lumumba?"

"Your little friend? He has been assigned a bunk in a children's tent. You can join him as soon as you are well." She shook her head in exasperation and returned to more critical patients.

The next morning, Sebu felt a little more like himself. The aid workers gradually fed him small portions of solid food, taking care not to overload his famished body. A starved person could die from too much nourishment at once, overburdening his weakened metabolism. He wandered through the bustling camp and tried to make sense of his new life. He passed the line for the food tent – it seemed completely unmoved since the last time he was there. Then he slipped through a mob, swarming an armored U.N. vehicle, with blue helmeted peacekeepers handing out care packages of soap and socks. He made his way through a makeshift marketplace, with people haggling over ration cards, used clothes and other necessities. That seemed a little exciting, but he had nothing to trade.

Sebu reached a jerry-built soccer field and his heart soared. He looked longingly at the kids playing rough. He knew he could have once run circles around them, but he peered down at his frail body and it was clear that he was still in no condition to join. He hadn't come so far only to be broken apart playing ball.

That night he settled into an "unattended minors" tent with Lumumba. They shared a bunk, crammed alongside many other orphans. Some of them tossed and mumbled through nightmares. Most played and whispered amongst themselves, eluding sleep and the certainty of nightmares. Sebu, Lumumba and a couple others played with a tattered deck of cards.

They felt an uneasy freedom in this microcosm, devoid of adult supervision. It seemed eerie that no one was there to tell them what to do. Given the power vacuum, there had already been quite a lot of jockeying and several skirmishes to establish the pecking order. Egos were bruised and noses were bloodied.

Sebu and Lumumba were still in no state to scrap, so they let the other boys feel tough for the moment. They gladly accepted the rotted, rickety bunks they were given and kept their heads down, content to hang with the other low-status newcomers.

The boys were just quietly killing time when a band of para-military rebels burst into the tent. They filed into a line, standing taut at attention. The children were petrified with fear. Had they escaped the annihilation of their villages, only to be gunned down under the protection of the blue helmets?

Sebu scanned the line of soldiers and was mystified to see how young they were. The oldest appeared to be in his twenties, but a couple of them were even younger than Sebu. Their uniforms were irregular, but relatively clean. The outfits were a source of pride – even the smallest soldier boy looked imperiously down at the tattered orphans. He had an assault rifle strapped to his shoulder. It was almost as large as he was.

The sight of the weapon lit a fire in Sebu. He wished he could have had the font of destructive power in his hands, on that horrific day, so he could have protected his loved ones from those demon men.

The miniature warrior stiffened and stretched himself as tall as he could, then barked: "At-ten-tion!" The orphans jumped out of their skin. The assembled rebels scowled at them until they took the hint. Boys roused each other from bed, to stand in a line across from those terrifying fighters – anything to halt their withering glares.

And then Commander Moses charged in with gusto, oozing machismo. He couldn't have been too deep into his twenties, but his angular face projected wisdom and leadership. He was tall and muscular. The orphans instantly wanted to be him. The entire tent had fallen pin-drop silent.

"At ease," he whispered. The boys slumped back into their natural slouches, like the air had been let out of them. Command-er Moses was a snake charmer.

"My brothers," his voice started a slow build, "we have all suffered. I have seen my sisters raped and my family murdered. I have seen my village burned to the ground. I have been a refugee and I have lived in camps just like this one. I was very angry. Are *you* angry?

A feral wail of agreement bubbled up from the orphans. Moses hit a nerve. They previously thought they were just sad, downtrodden and defeated; but now they realized they were furious. And their rage gave them unity and strength.

"Makanga is a cancer. He will destroy us all to fatten his belly with profits from our land." Commander Moses' face was twisted in anger and all the boys snarled along with him.

"I made a choice. I chose not to live like an animal in a cage, taking handouts from the United Nations and rotting in the dirt. I chose to fight. I chose to take back my homeland. Makanga's forces are very strong. The People's Rebellion needs every man, woman and child to band together, in order to defeat him. Do not worry that you are too small and weak. You are not!"

He strutted over to that pint-sized fighter and patted him on the shoulder. "Private Mosquito killed fourteen of Makanga's largest men." The kid beamed with pride. The orphans' jaws dropped in awe. Moses took the rifle from him and held it in the air. Private mosquito discreetly rubbed his shoulder, secretly relieved to be unburdened of its heft. "With AK-47, we are all equal!" Above his head, the battered weapon looked magnificent. They saw it as the source of their salvation – giving power to the powerless.

"I want to kill the bastards!" A child in the back blurted his feelings.

"That's the spirit!" Moses roared. "Boys, you have a choice. Waste away here, impotent and useless, or join the fight! Our trucks leave tomorrow at midnight for training camp. And don't you dare say a word to the white people. We were never here."

The rebels slipped out and disappeared into the night, leaving the orphans speechless and in awe. A moment later, the kids burst into excited speculation. They had a choice to make – but from their perspective it wasn't much of a choice. Sebu looked to Lumumba and for the first time since the massacre, he cracked a tiny smile.

11

Kaufman was back at that same nightclub of decadent desperation. What frightened him this time was that it took far less arm
twisting from the traders to get him there. He needed a break
after spending the last sixteen hours with his face buried in his
monitors – developing an options valuation model, analyzing de-
fault risk in emerging market bonds, researching the effects of
interventionist monetary policy on demand for distressed debt –
anything to distract him from the elephant in the room. But he
was starting to bore himself.

Kaufman had frittered his life away calculating risks. He
had painted himself into a sanitized corner, hedging against every
liability, but now he felt stagnant. Perhaps the greatest risk of all
was never taking one.

His days followed a familiar algorithm – wake, cocoa puffs,
news, subway, grind the day away with the pixelated glow of
screens against his face, subway, dinner, sleep, wake, cocoa puffs...

He glanced across the room – the traders were back to their
shameless pickup routines and the out-of-work models still ate them
up. He might as well have been watching the Discovery Channel:

The male of the species telegraphs his worth in a series of grandiose
courtship displays. He wears expensive clothes to demonstrate his wealth and
power. Any female would be lucky to invest her precious eggs in him. He
buys her overpriced cocktails to exhibit his financial security and to impair

her judgment. The female enhances her fertility and genetic fitness indicators with the help of cosmetics and corrective undergarments. They feel each other out, performing an intricate social dance to assess the authenticity of their mating signals. Will this pairing culminate in fertilization?

A sloppy drunk model danced and flailed so wildly she spilled out of the trader dog pile and fell into Kaufman's lap.

"Hello, sssailor!" She slurred, enveloping Kaufman in a boozy mist. He could light her breath on fire. Her eyes were glassy and she didn't know Kaufman from Adam. But he knew her.

"Hi, Carrie," Kaufman sighed. He noticed red lipstick smudged against her porcelain teeth and beads of perspiration breaking through a thick layer of foundation.

"Yeah, that's my name! This is t-te-terrif..."

"Tedious?"

She play slapped him. "Terrific. What's your name?" She traced her sweaty finger down his face, then suddenly heaved, leaned over and voided her stomach into an ice bucket.

Kaufman grabbed his phone and hit the speed dial. "Milos, I'll go."

Carrie was already snoring in his lap.

12

Private Mosquito savored his fleeting stint as commander, leading the column of orphan recruits in the dead of night, slithering on their bellies through the sleepy camp and crawling through a hole he had dug under the electrified fence. The blue helmets had heightened security when they heard of the rebels' infiltration the night before.

A rickety flatbed truck waited in the shadows just outside the perimeter. In a final flourish as ranking officer, Private Mosquito stage whispered, "Welcome to the rebellion, boys! Now get on the transport. That is an order!" The orphans clamored over each other to secure their places on their ride with destiny.

The truck bed was coated in a layer of fuzzy mold that turned to slime when they sat on it. Sebu guessed the vehicle was previously employed to transport fruit.

The diesel engine roared to life, belching smoke and the truck rumbled over pitted earth. No one in the camp would ever notice the children missing from the throngs of gaping mouths to feed.

Sebu and Lumumba sat in the back of the truck together, watching the refugee camp recede into history. They vowed to never be refugees again. They were willing to live or die by the gun, rather than subsist on their knees, groveling for charity. They had nearly perished staggering away from their village, but now they were speeding right back, to a hidden base not far from their homeland.

"Do you think we'll see that rat, Makanga on the battle-field?" Lumumba whispered.

"I am sure of it. And I will kill him myself."

They drove all night and all day, stopping only to refuel. The boys were given meager rations of stale bread and dirty water and told to relieve themselves off the side of the speeding vehicle. Some grew motion sick from the relentless vibrations and vomited over the rail as well. They were hungry and angry, all crammed togeth-er on the slippery truck bed, breaking out in minor scuffles. The sun began to set, as the shuddering transport finally sputtered through the concertina wire of the rebel stronghold.

"This looks too familiar," Lumumba whispered. They had just crawled under one barbed gate only to drive through another. The truck screeched to a halt in a clearing in the center of the compound, abruptly jolting half the boys from sleep. The place looked as bleak as the refugee camp, but not nearly as crowd-ed. The perimeter was protected by guard towers, with swiv-el-mounted .50 caliber guns.

Commander Moses bounded out of his quarters, wild-eyed and foaming at the mouth. The orphans stiffened – had they done something wrong?

"Out! Get out you little vomit, pig shit, fleas! Your lives depend on your ability to follow orders and move fast!"

Moses' men leapt up on the truck bed and plucked the new re-cruits down onto the dirt. The transport roared away, leaving them choking on diesel fumes. The gate slammed shut behind them.

"How did you talk me into this?" Lumumba whispered.

"We must avenge our families." Sebu was unfazed.

Private Mosquito took Commander Moses' side. "At-ten-tion!" He barked, louder and prouder than ever.

The boys rose drowsily, forming a crooked line.

"Pathetic!" Moses sneered. His men forcefully prodded and rifle-butted the boys into tight formation.

Adult rebels lounged outside the officers' tent – drinking, smoking and enjoying the spectacle. Sebu looked to the battle-hardened warriors in awe. They all seemed so cool and confident, with their weapons resting casually on their shoulders – like they could go out and effortlessly kill their enemies all day and be back for a night of drinking and carousing.

Moses caught Sebu distracted and delivered a quick slap to his face. Sebu's attention snapped back to the lecture at hand.

"Let me demonstrate the first rule of The Rebellion. Desertion is treason! It risks the lives of your brothers and betrays our cause." The boys were shocked by Moses' virulence – this was not part of his sales pitch a couple nights before.

Three blindfolded men were dragged, moaning and trembling, in front of them. One man wet his pants.

"I am innocent!" He pleaded. Moses charged over without hesitation, pulled a 9mm pistol from his waistband and drove a round through the prisoner's forehead. It erupted from the back of his skull, spraying brain and bone fragments on the orphans. A few of the kids felt their own warm urine trickle down their legs.

"That is what happens to deserters!" The Commander roared. A boy fainted out of formation. Soldiers were already primed to dump a bucket of water on his face and pull him back up in line.

Sebu was nauseous and confused, but he buried his feelings.

Moses executed the other two hooded men with the same dispassionate precision. Their corpses cooled as the rebel leader turned to his new recruits.

"Your first job is to bury these pigs." Moses turned and strutted to his quarters without looking back.

The boys carried out their order in solemn silence, trying to avert their eyes from the dead men's faces. They all wished they had stayed in the refugee camp. Sebu fulfilled his obligation like a machine – he sent his mind elsewhere, to his family and to his thirst for retribution.

"Do you think they're really deserters?" Lumumba mumbled in Sebu's ear.

"I don't know. Let's just do as we're told and live to take revenge."

Once the bloody business was over, the boys were shown to their quarters. They were assigned cots in a tent not unlike the one they left behind the night before. They felt exhausted, like the walking dead, but none dared face the horrors that would meet them in their dreams.

Commander Moses stepped in and looked them over, nodding in satisfaction. As much as they despised him, they had already developed an inexplicable yearning for his approval.

"I know you hate me now. That is fine. I do not need your love. I need your obedience. It's the only way you will endure this. It's the only way we can defeat him."

He beckoned Mosquito in to pass out bottles of rotgut. "Drink this when you want to forget your troubles – or when you need a shot of courage in battle." The boys forced the hooch down their throats, puckering and coughing in disgust. Most had never had a drink before. But they welcomed the mind-dulling buzz.

Sebu abstained and when he saw Lumumba lift the bottle to his lips, he shook his head. Lumumba nodded and put the bottle down. They would keep their eyes clear through this ordeal.

Before sunrise, the hungover boys were slave-driven to run endless laps around the perimeter. With throbbing heads, they sweated out the poison they had swallowed the night before. Predictably enough,

Sebu and Lumumba led the pack and Moses took note of their fleet-footedness. Once the children were drained of all their strength, Mosquito called them back to fall in line. The new recruits teetered in their rows, drenched in sweat, dizzy and panting under the beating sun. Moses paced back and forth, assessing the ranks.

"I'll make soldiers out of you after all." The Commander's words were like honey to them. A flood of dopamine washed their aches away. Their hearts and minds entangled tighter into Moses' grasp. He pushed and pulled, dangled the carrot and brandished the stick. Sebu felt himself being lulled. He bit his lip hard, and made a silent promise not to let himself be brainwashed.

The orphans could not contain their excitement when they were issued their assault rifles. Their weapons were battered, but carefully maintained. They smelled of fresh grease.

"The AK-47 is not a toy," Moses professed, "It is the most effective killing machine in the world. Designed over sixty years ago, it has stood the test of time. It was used by more armies in more wars than any other rifle. It is simple enough that even a child can kill with it. It is so robust that you can drop it in the mud, but still pick it up and discharge thirty bullets in under five seconds."

Sebu handled his weapon reverently, pulling back the bolt, examining the magazine, clicking through the fire settings. He had a preternatural understanding of the rifle. He ran his fingers along the grain of the wooden stock, familiarized himself with every nick and scratch on the weapon. Sebu wondered how many lives his seasoned gun had ended, how many conflicts it had seen and how many times it changed hands. Perhaps it was pulled from the cold carcass of one of his enemies.

Another boy couldn't control himself and treated his weapon like a plaything. He pretended to gun down his friend, making rat-a-tat noises with his mouth. Commander Moses glowed with anger and pistol-whipped his face. The boy fell to the ground, bleeding from the mouth. He held back tears and spit out a tooth.

"I told you it's not a toy. Treat your weapon with respect. Never point it at something you don't intend to kill."

The boy flushed with shame and wiped the blood from his lips. The other children hugged their weapons tight against their chests, already forming a security-blanket bond with their guns.

Confined to the base, Sebu's world narrowed to a pinpoint. He slept, he ate, he trained and he dreamt of nothing beyond the day he would tear Makanga's head from his body. His hands grew calloused and so did his heart.

Day after day, the children were rudely awoken at dawn, sometimes with barked orders, sometimes with gunfire – to inoculate them from fear, to make them sleep lightly, so they could be ready to fight and kill at a moment's notice.

They were each given a small bowl of gruel and exactly sixty seconds to eat it. If they couldn't finish in time, their spoons were yanked out of their mouths. They had to learn to nourish themselves quickly, since there were no lunch breaks in the heat of battle.

They ran lap after lap, until their legs were striated with sinuous muscle, until they could relentlessly chase down an enemy and wait for him to tire out. If he collapsed in exhaustion, they could swarm like piranhas and tear him limb from limb.

The tiniest boy, named Innocent, ran barefoot. The supply closet didn't have boots even remotely small enough to fit his doll feet. He tried tying larger boots tight around his ankles, but they just caused blisters and flew off at inopportune times.

The boys practiced hand-to-hand combat, disarming each other, twisting wrists, using leverage, forcing submissions. They learned the most efficient ways to kill with a blade – the stabbing and slashing targets that would cause the quickest blood loss and organ failure. They were taught to be ruthless and unrelenting, pummeling the enemy and capitalizing on his weaknesses. Tall, lanky Lumumba was particularly good at wrestling and weaseling out of holds.

Sebu was the star of the gun range, outshining even the adult rebels. While some boys waited until Moses was occupied, then squandered their daily ammo allowance enjoying the thrill of fully-automatic fire; Sebu shot one round at time, making every bullet count. He had an innate understanding of ballistics. Unprompted, he figured out how to compensate for the effects of wind speed and gravity on his bullets' trajectory. The Kalashnikov AK-47 was not the most accurate weapon, but Sebu handled his like a sniper.

The orphans spent their nights in a haze, guzzling moonshine and snorting brown-brown, a mixture of cocaine and gunpowder that made their brains addled and fearless. They were forced to sing propaganda songs and were blessed by witch doctors, who granted them "invincibility" in battle. Having a head full of drugs and no real combat experience, they eagerly bought into the lies. Sebu and Lumumba pantomimed the binging, but maintained their solemn vow of purity, both from snorting narcotics and from swallowing nonsense.

After weeks of waking up to cacophony and running around in circles on empty stomachs, the boys yearned to break the monotony. They thought they were ready to fight. They were hungrier than ever for revenge.

One day, Sebu made bulls-eyes of all thirty rounds in his mag. Commander Moses strutted over, genuinely impressed.

"Sebu."

"Yes, Commander?" He barked, as he was trained to do.

"You will lead a child platoon." Moses turned and walked away, leaving Sebu dumbfounded. The children were all impressed by Sebu's skill, but would they really take his orders?

That night, the orphans were fast asleep, clinging to the few brief hours in which nothing was demanded of them.

Commander Moses barged in and growled: "Wake up!"

The children sprang to attention, hazy and confused.

"The big soldiers are going to raid an enemy village. These villagers are allied with Makanga. They betrayed us all. We will punish them with death and take their supplies."

He strolled through the tent, eyeing his child soldiers. "I have selected this, the best of the child platoons, to join in our attack. We will surround the village and destroy them. Everyone will shoot together, then this platoon will stay back to cover the big soldiers when we charge in."

The children's hearts pounded in fear and exhilaration.

"Sebu is your Platoon Leader. An order from him is the same as an order from me." Sebu's stomach fluttered in excitement. The other children looked to him with newfound respect.

"I don't have shoes," Innocent peeped sheepishly from the back of the room.

"Soon you will. You will take them from the feet of the enemy."

13

Kaufman shuttled across the Atlantic at nearly the speed of sound. Milos had packed him off in the Jupiter Fund's Gulfstream jet. He was enveloped in floor to ceiling mahogany and leather, sinking into a plush recliner that made him feel like he was floating on a cloud.

But Kaufman was a wreck. How did one address an African Warlord? He read the man's dossier, which Sterling passed along from one of his contacts in Langley:

Makanga had been educated in the United States. He spent four years shivering at snowy Rutgers University, dodged a date-rape allegation and graduated with honors. He returned home to claim an officer post his influential father finagled for him in the Zaire Army. He rose rapidly through the ranks, distinguishing himself through acts of bravery and skullduggery in the Congo Wars, but was eventually ousted along with President Sese Seko Mobutu.

Zaire became The Democratic Republic of the Congo and Makanga brooded, plotted and waited for his window of opportunity to claw his way back to power. He was determined to seize his share of the natural treasures buried across the land. The place had descended into anarchy and there were plenty of power vacuums to be filled by anyone willing to grease some palms and hack some limbs.

The psychological profile depicted him as a psychopath — not the obvious kind, like a serial killer in a b-movie. Real psychopaths made up about two percent of the population and an even greater proportion of people in power. They could seem perfectly affable and simulate normal human emotion, yet deep down they were incapable of empathy, lied whenever it was convenient, acted recklessly and ultimately felt no remorse. These traits seemed just as applicable to someone else Kaufman knew.

Kaufman knew he would have to maintain his clear-eyed, professional detachment. But in the meantime, he raided Milos' liquor cabinet to settle his nerves. He sunk back into the buttery leather, taking refuge in a bottle of thirty year old scotch.

Milos' regular flight attendant wasn't aboard – the fewer people who knew about this expedition, the better. If Kaufman were licensed, he'd have been asked to fly the plane himself. They had told the traders that he was taking an extended vacation, eliciting groans and protestations. Who would hand-feed them plum trading setups? They would be forced to think for themselves. Not even Kaufman's parents knew where he was going – only that he wouldn't always be available by phone and it was probably best to email.

Alone in the opulent, soundproof cabin, Kaufman eventually dozed off. He didn't wake until the jet made a rough landing on a dusty airstrip in the middle of nowhere.

He groggily debarked and the pilot obeyed his order to refuel and take off again without asking questions.

Kaufman stood alone on the dirty airstrip, jetlagged and disoriented, clutching a small Tumi suitcase and sweating through his shirt. He spotted a low-slung office at the other end of the runway, rippling in the heat haze. He padded across the melting tarmac in a daze.

Inside, he took his place at the end of a short queue of discreet "business travelers," that might as well have been an Interpol lineup. Kaufman felt a fleeting gust of relief every time the rotary fan swiveled by, only to be broiled again the second it passed.

He reached a wiry customs agent, swimming in a baggy uniform, who looked down at him from a lofted Formica desk. The sickly man inspected Kaufman's American passport with an entrepreneurial glint in his eye.

"What is the reason for your visit?"

"Tourism," Kaufman deadpanned.

The agent snickered incredulously. "May I see your entry visa?"

"I was told I don't need one."

"You certainly do. It takes four weeks to obtain."

Kaufman saw where this conversation was going, but he played through the motions. "The web site said I don't..."

The customs crook leaned in to whisper: "I can expedite your application for one hundred U.S. dollars."

"I'll give you five," Kaufman sighed.

"Very good, sir!" The man just doubled his daily income.

Kaufman rolled his eyes and reached into his pocket. He held out the cash and the poor man almost grasped it, but he heard a commotion across the room.

"No, no, no!" A pair of Makanga's burly envoys called out.

The bureaucrat panicked and withdrew his hand. "Sir, I cannot take such gifts. But thank you for offering and have a pleasant stay."

"Mr. Kaufman, please come with us." Makanga's goons had muscles bulging through their dark suits. They were already breathing down his neck. Kaufman was spooked. He wished he could just bribe the man and take a cab.

14

Sebu's platoon slunk stealthily through the foliage, some of them with RPG tubes strapped to their backs. Their heads swam with anxiety and excitement. They itched for their first taste of battle and repressed nagging fears of their own mortality. Moses told them the ambush was meticulously planned and victory would be certain. But what if something went awry? What if they were so nervous that their arms would tremble and their aim would fail? What if they were blindly walking into a trap? What if all the big soldiers were killed and the children were captured and tortured? Would they stay strong and spit in the face of death, or buckle and betray the secret location of their base?

A couple boys took slugs of hooch to steady their trembling hands, but Sebu insisted that they moderate their intake: "Your mind must be sharp, my brothers. We are so close to avenging our families. There must be no mistakes."

They reached the outskirts and crouched, aiming their rifles at the village. The adult platoons were already in similar formations, hidden behind trees, encircling the perimeter in a stranglehold. The enemy would not escape.

Commander Moses winked at Sebu from across the line. The boy shuddered – he had never really trusted Moses, but now he sensed something especially shifty in his eyes.

Sebu peered at the villagers, trying to spot Makanga's loy-alists. He saw children playing, women hunched over steaming pots or grinding out their housework. Where were the men? Per-haps they were in cahoots with the warlord? No, he saw a few men – one carrying fish from the river, another hammering away on a hut. They seemed like the same peaceful neighbors Sebu had grown up with.

"Where is the enemy?" Lumumba puzzled.

"Not here," Sebu was certain. He turned to his subordinates. "These are not soldiers. When he says 'fire,' shoot your guns into the dirt."

"We must kill the enemy," a brainwashed boy insisted.

"Look at them," Sebu whispered urgently. "These people might as well be our mothers and fathers, brothers and sisters. They are not warriors – they are like us."

The children looked torn. What kind of lousy soldiers refused their first real order? They were so hungry to finally prove themselves.

"Commander Moses will kill us!" The same boy protested.

"This is an order. So he will just kill me."

The orphans hesitated.

"Imagine murdering them," Sebu exploded. "Picture them crying out in pain and dying at your feet? Will you be able to live the rest of your life in peace, knowing what you did?"

"Fire!" Moses shouted from across the line, ending any debate.

The rebels unleashed hell, their automatic weapons tearing the villagers to pieces, indiscriminately mowing down men, wom-en and children in mechanized slaughter. It was all too painfully familiar. Sebu's boys were horrified and they fired into the dirt.

"Charge!" Moses led the grownups headfirst, killing, pil-laging and raping. Sebu could do nothing but look on in shock, as the rebels mercilessly turned human beings into inanimate ob-jects, grinding them up into bloody offal. Sebu realized the rebels

were no better than Makanga's men. Perhaps they had some twisted rhetoric to justify their actions, but ultimately they were just
killing and stealing to keep their war machine fueled.

"Retreat," Sebu ordered in disgust.

"What?!" Another child gasped.

"We cannot save them." Sebu sprang up and led them to the
refuge of the trees.

In the distance, Commander Moses looked up from his
bloody harvest to see Sebu's platoon withdraw. Rage crossed his
eyes. He lifted his rifle to cut Sebu down, but his forehead erupted
in a crimson bloom and his lifeless bulk collapsed in the dirt.

Dead-eye Sebu lowered his smoking weapon. "Let's get out
of here." The children escaped together into the jungle, leaving the
carnage behind them. Sebu knew he was taking responsibility for
his brothers and prayed he wasn't leading them all to their deaths.

Innocent looked down, frustrated at his blistered feet.

15

The envoys deposited Kaufman in the back of their Range Rover and stonewalled him throughout the bumpy ride. There wasn't much road to speak of. Kaufman's stomach churned as thrashed shock absorbers struggled to negotiate relentless pits and craters.

The scenery was so lush and verdant that Kaufman wished he was there under different circumstances. The Congo could have been a natural paradise, but human beings had a tendency to ruin things. Kaufman noticed his handlers seemed very tense. What did they know that he didn't? He tried to break the ice.

"Will General Makanga..."

"President Makanga," the driver corrected.

"He's President now?"

The goon grunted in the affirmative.

An awkward silence lasted several minutes, and Kaufman's imagination raced ahead of him. He realized he had no idea who these men really were. For all he knew, they could be Makanga's enemies, sent to intercept and murder him. They could bury his body deep in the jungle and it would never be found.

"So uh, how long have you lived in the D.R.C.?" Kaufman tried to get them talking about themselves, to form a personal connection so they'd be less inclined to put a bullet in his brain.

"This is not the Democratic Republic of the Congo," the envoy insisted.

"Zaire, then?"

"No. President Makanga is the elected ruler of the sovereign state of Lualaba."

"Okay, why not..." Kaufman stifled a snicker.

"You had better watch your tone, boy! The President demands respect!" The passenger, who had thus far been silent, erupted. Kaufman's heart raced. Was this the part where they'd make him dig his own shallow grave, then hack his head off with a rusty machete?

The driver scolded the passenger in Tshiluba, which Kaufman didn't understand. They had a heated back-and-forth and Kaufman speculated that they were debating how best to dispose of his body. He considered leaping out of the speeding vehicle, but he figured at this velocity he'd probably splatter his brains against a tree.

The envoys' conversation came to a tense détente and the passenger turned back to look Kaufman in the eye.

"Mr. Kaufman, I apologize for my outburst. Please do not take it as a reflection on The President. He has instructed us to welcome you and treat you with the utmost hospitality," the envoy mumbled through gritted teeth. It pained him to humble himself to an insolent foreigner.

Kaufman felt his sphincter relax. He was granted at least a few more minutes above ground.

The Range Rover emerged from the jungle and stopped at a towering security gate. A heavily armed guard rapped the envoy's window, checked his papers and waved the Rover through. The vehicle rolled into a fortified compound, with concrete walls and guard towers manned by snipers. The modern battlements were built around a sprawling, colonial palace that stood in stark contrast. The manor house was wrapped in a colonnade, with sweeping arches and an ornamental roof. Kaufman figured it was constructed by one of King Leopold's governors, in the days of the Belgian occupation.

The envoys led Kaufman to the lavish entryway and were grateful to pass him along to burden someone else. All the various handlers had been apprised that their well-being was predicated on his.

A white-gloved butler opened the wrought-iron door for Kaufman. He apprehensively peeked into an expansive foyer, adorned with carved elephant tusks and staffed by a small army of smiling, uniformed domestics.

"Welcome!" The butler announced. The servants all stopped what they were doing and bowed and curtsied in unison. Kaufman squirmed as they scrutinized him behind plastic smiles.

"Hi," he muttered sheepishly. From the corner of his eye, he spotted a couple guards standing at attention in the hallway, holding submachine guns across their chests. They might as well have been statues. The butler forced his attention back to the pleasantries:

"We have been asked to make your stay here as comfortable as possible. President Makanga told us that Mr. Kaufman, of the Jupiter Fund, is our most welcome guest."

"Uh, thanks. Where is the President?"

"He is attending to matters of state, but he shall be back to dine with you this evening. Niambi, please show Mr. Kaufman to his quarters."

A bell-boy reached for Kaufman's case.

"I'm fine, thanks."

The boy withdrew his hand, seemingly insulted.

Niambi was a statuesque woman in a fitted suit. She sashayed over and smiled at Kaufman, her eyes smoldering and suggestive. She tilted her head in the direction of his room. Kaufman followed her swishing hips up the stairs, sneaking another nervous peek at the poker-faced men with assault weapons.

Niambi led Kaufman into his sunny, gilded suite and pointed to the phone. "You may order room service at any time." She handed him a scented calling card. "And if you need me for anything – anything at all, do not hesitate to call."

Niambi looked Kaufman straight in the eye, making certain he fully understood. Kaufman smiled politely. He wouldn't let himself be caught in Makanga's honeytrap.

She glided out, leaving Kaufman bewildered.

"How 'bout some life insurance?" He mumbled under his breath.

16

Sebu hacked through dense vegetation, clearing a path for his child platoon. The jungle teemed with millions of different species of plants, animals and insects. Every few paces had a unique combination of flora and fauna, some yet undiscovered by human beings. Sebu led his boys trampling through myriads of distinct microcosms, filled with strange sights, sounds and smells. They were trekking through their own backyards, but so much of the jungle was still strange and unfamiliar to them. Of course the boys were too preoccupied to fully appreciate the splendor.

Sebu stopped and took a knee, dug in his pack for a tattered map and checked it against his tin compass.

"Vengeance is near, my brothers." He sprung up and forged onward with renewed vigor. But the others lumbered listlessly.

"I'm hungry," Innocent whined. Most of the boys chimed in, echoing the sentiment.

"Eat your field rations," Sebu sighed. The rebels had given them jars of gruel and a few knotty potatoes.

"I ate them all," Innocent whimpered.

"What?! I told you we must save food."

"I was starving." The other boys broke out in agreement.

Sebu halted and turned irritably to his troops.

"My brothers, we must be disciplined. Our enemies are so powerful and we are so few. We cannot waste time crying over our bellies. We must be willing to go with less, to need nothing, to push ourselves harder. We have to be smarter and quicker if we want to survive. Makanga's forces are a poisonous snake. Our only chance is cut off the head. We must take him by surprise."

The boys cheered and pushed themselves through hunger. But willpower could only go so far. Sebu led them off course, to a place he did not want to go.

A few stomach-growling hours later, Lumumba caught on: "Please don't take us there." He felt his legs locking up on him. Every muscle fiber in his body was committed to staying away.

"We need food," Sebu implored.

"I can't go back, my brother." Lumumba pleaded, his face strained in desperation, his eyes watering. Lumumba felt his breathing quicken and his heart race. His hands became clammy and his body cooked itself into a fever.

"What choice do we have? Would you rather starve?" Sebu's voice cracked. He wanted nothing more than to grant Lumumba's wish, but they wouldn't last much longer without sustenance. On an intellectual level, Lumumba knew Sebu was right. But that didn't mean much in the vortex of a panic attack.

Sebu embraced his friend and all the boys followed suit, enveloping him in brotherhood. The children knew what kind of sacrifice he was going to make for them. They would have been petrified to do the same.

Sebu could not afford to share Lumumba's pain. He had taken responsibility for all of them, so his own feelings had to be ignored.

Lumumba and the boys followed Sebu into the scorched ruins of his village. The clearing had overgrown with switchgrass and the charred huts had crumbled to the ground. Corpses were picked clean of flesh, bones bleached in the sun. But the miasma of fire and death was strong as ever. Most of the boys had never been there, but even they burst into tears. It might as well have been their villages – for they all suffered the same fate.

"Dig through the church. There should still be a food cellar in the ground." Sebu pointed to the wreckage in the center of town. The boys ran to it, like moths to a flame, tunneling their vision to block out everything but their desperate yearning for nourishment. They climbed over debris and sidestepped skeletons twisted in poses of agony.

Lumumba stayed back and turned to Sebu. "Let us honor our families." Sebu solemnly nodded.

Lumumba dug holes until his fingers bled, then laid his parents and brother to rest in the unforgiving earth. Sebu could only find his mother's remains and tearfully buried them near the ashes of the family hut. They prayed for the souls of their lost relatives and for the strength to strike down their nemesis.

The other boys hit pay dirt with the underground cellar of the church still intact. They unearthed cassava and tubers, old and scorched by the blast, but still edible. They bit into onions and relished them as if they were apples. They filled their sacks with food and brought some to their grieving commanders.

Sebu was compelled to keep digging – he wanted to honor all his neighbors, but Sebu pulled him away. "We have our mission. They would have wanted vengeance as well."

17

The butler led anxious Kaufman into a sprawling, African Black-wood paneled dining hall lined with oil paintings of Congolese prehistory. The table was set with mirror-polished silver and priceless colonial-era china. A string-quartet played Kaufman's favorite composition by François Couperin. Apparently Milos wasn't the only one with spies in his pocket.

Kaufman was ushered to the tail of the table, surrounded by smiling dignitaries – some in sharp, western suits and others wearing traditional African robes. Kaufman wondered if they served any purpose beyond lending the general a thin patina of respectability. They came across a little too perfect; like they were handpicked and groomed to look like some kind of Congolese nobility. For all Kaufman knew, they could have been vagrants with stately faces, garbed in fancy costumes. The ersatz dignitaries nodded eagerly.

Kaufman flashed a nervous smile. From the moment he touched down, Makanga's people were all trying too hard. Kaufman smelled desperation. If this was really such a sweet deal, they wouldn't have to sell it to him – the opportunity would sell itself. Kaufman resolved to be as polite and terse as possible, then high-tail it off the continent at his earliest opportunity.

The quartet abruptly halted in mid-melody to punch out a bombastic fanfare. Makanga strutted in wearing his most flamboyant dress uniform. The dignitaries rose at his presence, feigning religious ecstasy and Kaufman awkwardly stood after them. He marveled at Makanga's size – almost a head taller, with an extra hundred pounds of muscle. His massive chest swelled and contracted as he breathed. Even the muscles in his beastly jaw flexed and rippled, like he was always primed to bite.

Makanga sat at the head of the table, then gestured cordially for everyone to sit. His hawkish eyes locked on Kaufman and his brow furrowed. The dignitaries turned to Kaufman and mirrored the same expression. Kaufman squirmed under their collective gaze.

"You are Mr. Kaufman, of the Jupiter Fund?" Makanga sounded incredulous. Who was this child Milos Sterling had the effrontery to send him? The Greek chorus of lackeys disdainfully sucked their teeth.

"Yes, sir," Kaufman stammered.

"You look young." Makanga did not beat around the bush.

For a moment that felt like an eternity, Kaufman was at a loss for words. Was he expected to defend his credentials? All eyes narrowed, scrutinizing him.

"As do you, Mr. President." Kaufman forced a chuckle.

Makanga burst out in a laugh that echoed through the room. His sycophants followed suit. Kaufman exhaled in relief – he knew he had to at least feign interest and respect. If Makanga knew he had nothing to gain from Kaufman, he might not be so inclined to keep him comfortable; or alive, for that matter.

"I shot you a boar!" Makanga declared, to the audible delight of the guests.

"I'm honored," Kaufman gulped.

Makanga waved his hand and a tuxedoed waiter flamboyantly marched in carrying a colossal roast on a silver tray, placing it directly in front of Kaufman. He looked down at the blackened beast, with eyes gouged but tusks still intact. The smell of seared pork assaulted Kaufman's nostrils. This was clearly not the ideal time for Kaufman to admit he was a vegetarian. And if his Yiddish mama saw the trafe he was about to ingest, she may have thrown a fit; but for the sake of diplomacy, Kaufman steeled his stomach for nausea.

He noticed the actors eyeing his boar with hungry, watering mouths. Didn't Makanga feed them? All it took was a whiff of meat to crack their composure. Kaufman wished he could slip them his portion. They clearly needed it more than he did.

The waiter cut him a generous slice. Everyone watched intently to gauge Kaufman's enjoyment. He made an awkward show of savoring it and they all nodded in approval. Kaufman saw one of the luminaries – an old man in a dashiki – close his eyes and subtly lick his lips in anticipation of his share. But to Kaufman, the cooked flesh smelled and tasted like sewage sliding down his throat.

"Meet our new corporate sponsor!" Makanga proclaimed, as if Kaufman had passed some perverse test. The luminaries chuckled. "Mr. Kaufman reports back to Milos Sterling himself." They nodded in vigorous approval, as if it meant something to them, all the while darting sideways glances at the boar.

"Tomorrow we will visit some mines and you shall see what bountiful wealth our land has to offer!" Makanga beamed.

Kaufman nodded politely, struggling to wash the taste of death from his mouth.

18

A serpentine convoy of vehicles idled in front of Makanga's estate, belching clouds of black diesel smoke; rumbling engines engulfing the compound in a low, ominous growl. A jeep, mounted with a Browning .50 caliber machine gun led the column, followed by an armored Humvee packed with mercenaries, succeeded by a vintage Mercedes limousine and another gun-mounted jeep taking up the rear. More soldiers of fortune swarmed the convoy on motorcycles.

Makanga and his entourage led Kaufman through the choking exhaust and unnerving reverberation, into the relative quiet of the bulletproofed limo. The general sat unnervingly close by Kaufman's side, with menacing bodyguards lurking across from them. They stared at Kaufman the same way they were paid to watch everyone – with paranoid suspicion – in case he was really some foreign agent sent to assassinate their meal ticket.

"You will find our operation is a model of efficiency," Makanga already started back in on the hard sell.

"That's what I like to hear." Kaufman fidgeted.

The convoy roared out the gate, kicking up clouds of dust in its wake.

The house servants let out a collective sigh of relief, that they would enjoy a few hours without the constant threat of castigation.

Kaufman peered through the window at the dense jungle rolling by.

"Is my country not beautiful?" Makanga wouldn't afford him an instant of quiet contemplation.

"Yes, it's lovely. Though I haven't seen much of it yet."

"Don't worry, we shall show you all the highlights."

"In truth, I'm just as interested in the low-lights."

The bodyguards glared. They hoped Kaufman would fall out of Makanga's favor, so they could have their fun.

Makanga frowned and Kaufman promptly regretted his candor. "They are few and far between." Makanga forced a smug grin.

Kaufman nodded, just as they passed a man with stumps for arms, struggling to pull the rope of an emaciated cow with his teeth. The cow looked just as bitter as the man who was dragging her. Kaufman darted a glance at the general, who pretended not to notice the squalor.

The convoy reached another barbed barrier, manned by yet another complement of uniformed thugs. They peeked into the vehicles for the obligatory security check, then parted the gates for the man who signed the checks.

Makanga gestured to the guards. "We have contracted with a South African security firm called Tactical Outcomes. They are the most professional private army in all of Africa."

"Mercenaries?"

"Yes, trained by an American – a former Green Beret."

Kaufman wondered where the syndicate had dug up all these hulking, battle-scarred warriors. Perhaps they scoured the armies of the African continent, poaching the most ruthless terminators, skimming the cream of the martial ranks. Or maybe they just sprung them all from jail.

The column of vehicles snaked down the narrow, winding path cut into the side of the hill, flattening any plant or animal in its way. The oversized chassis hugged the wall of the mountain to avoid rolling off a cliff. They reached the mining operation, sprawling across the side of the river near Sebu's decimated village. The surrounding trees had been hacked to stumps, and severe-faced mercenaries guarded heaping barrels of coltan in covered huts. The valley resounded with the growl of combusting diesel.

The men cut their engines, and for a few moments everything was silent, save for an occasional groan coming from the bank of the river. Kaufman, Makanga and his sham cabinet stepped out of the limo and walked to the water's edge.

Several deep pits had been carved out of the softened ground near the water. Teams of wiry, shirtless miners strained and sweated in the sun, shoveling mud from the bottoms of the pits into water basins, where other broken men sloshed the mud around, sifting the ore from the earth.

"Our production is increasing daily. We may even have to curtail supply, so prices will remain high," Makanga beamed.

Kaufman peered at the emaciated workers, toiling and wincing, their blood boiling in the heat. "How are they paid?"

"You need not worry about these men. The average Congolese worker makes the equivalent of ten U.S. Dollars a week. Our miners make twice as much a day."

The slaves kept shoveling away, pretending they didn't notice the costumed circus leaning over them in their holes.

A couple pits over, a guard pointed his rifle and barked down at unseen laborers inside. Kaufman shuddered. Makanga flashed the merc a nasty look, which seemed to instill great fear in him.

Kaufman had assumed his discomfort would eventually plateau, but he grew progressively more anxious with every passing moment. He counted the seconds until he could hop the next jet home. Kaufman imagined prostrating himself and kissing the tarmac at JFK.

"Mind if I take a mud sample?" Kaufman had no idea why, but it seemed like an appropriate gesture – to go through the motions of due diligence.

"By all means!" Makanga motioned flamboyantly toward the riverbank, as if to project confidence in the richness of his soil.

Kaufman stepped gingerly to the water's edge and pulled a plastic container out of his pocket. He bent over to scoop a little bit of the Congo into his tube.

Makanga and his lackeys stared intently, trying to gauge Kaufman's interest. Would the boy speak favorably of them to the financial goliath in New York? Would Milos Sterling anoint them with backing and legitimacy, so Makanga could become the absolute ruler of the province?

WHOOSH – three rocket propelled grenades roared low across the river, leaving neat trails of smoke in the air. One almost robbed Kaufman of his head.

Still crouching, he was petrified for a fraction of a moment that felt like an eternity – before he was consciously aware of what was happening. Time slowed down to a trickle. A hundred thoughts raced through his mind at once. His eyes darted fast like a rodent – first to the jungle on the other side of the river – no one was visible. He traced the trajectory of the shells.

KABOOM – concussions shook the earth beneath his feet. Kaufman dove face-first into the mud.

One shell missed and blew a crater out of empty earth, launching a deadly fountain of rocks and sludge into the air. The second tore the limousine into shards of flying metal. The third ignited a coltan hut, engulfing it in infernal fire.

Kaufman heard inhuman wails. His eyes shot back to the gutted limo. A couple diplomats were peppered with shrapnel, crying and bleeding all over themselves. One hapless man was gashed right through his femoral artery. His blood sprayed in a pressurized jet stream. Kaufman estimated he had roughly thirty seconds left to live.

The mercenaries moved as one rageful force, pointing their weapons and opening fire into the seemingly empty jungle. Their assault rifles spit bullets over the dignitaries' heads, across the river and into the dense foliage.

Makanga's bodyguards leapt onto the jeeps and swiveled their big guns toward the unseen enemy. The mounted weapons sucked in belts of armor-piercing tracer bullets and blasted thousands of heavy rounds across the river. Shell casings piled up in mounds of hot copper. A palm tree caught fire.

The soldier's faces were fixed in killer rage, the dignitaries cowered in fear and eventually all the weapons started overheating and running out of ammo.

The firing finally trickled to a stop. There was still no sign of life across the way.

The dignitaries cautiously stood. A guard walked over to tend to the wounded.

"They must be dead," Makanga announced, peeking out from behind a tree stump.

Kaufman sat upright. The dignitaries brushed the dirt off their tattered robes.

Kaufman was shocked to see a mere child emerge, like a flash from the smoldering jungle. Sebu was fast and agile. He appeared possessed. His eyes were locked on his foe. He sprinted to the water's edge and aimed his AK-47 at Makanga's head.

The mercenaries scrambled to reload and cycle their weapons as Sebu managed to squeeze off a single round in mid-gallop. It cut across the river and plunged into Makanga's shoulder, hurling him to the ground. Sebu dove back into the jungle, trailed by a volley of automatic weapon fire.

The whole platoon of child soldiers burst from behind trees and rocks, fingers heavy on their triggers, angry vengeance in their eyes. They savored this moment that they had bled, starved, suffered and trained so hard for. Each boy had fantasized about it in different ways, but nothing compared to the real thrill of seeing their enemies crushed by their own little hands. Makanga's forces had taken everything from them, without an ounce of remorse. Their childhoods were long gone. They had nothing left but thirst for revenge and they were now finally drinking their fill.

The mercenaries were pinned against the hill, lacking sufficient cover. Measly children were getting the better of them. Limbs were shot off and faces turned to mush.

"Retreat!" Makanga bellowed with primal fear in his voice. He had grown soft from a succession of turkey shoots, no longer accustomed to fighting people who shot back.

The general's bodyguards used the mercenaries' cover fire to herd Makanga, Kaufman and the surviving dignitaries into the jeeps, then sped away from the fray.

The children evaporated back into the jungle from whence they came. They giggled with glee as they sprinted away, through the twists and turns of the wilderness that Sebu and Lumumba knew so well.

Kaufman was shell-shocked, hyperventilating in the jeep. He could not even begin to process what had happened. Were Makanga and his fearsome fighters just bested by a troop of armed children? And what on earth were kids doing with machine guns? Kaufman felt like he had slipped into an alternate universe.

The driver was frantic and sloppy, bumping and bouncing over craters, exacerbating everyone's wounds.

A bodyguard tended to Makanga's hemorrhaging shoulder. The general panted in anger and pain. His diplomatic poise had entirely disappeared.

"When I find that boy, I will cut him to pieces! I will eat his heart!" Makanga roared.

Kaufman was reminded of an old saying – if you shoot a rhino, you'd better kill it; because nothing is more dangerous than an angry, wounded beast. He knew Makanga would chase that spectral boy to the end of the earth if necessary. He would not rest until the child was atomized, so not even his memory would remain.

Kaufman started to wonder if he'd make it home alive.

19

A sour silence consumed the dining hall. Kaufman, Makanga and the dignitaries were all cleaned and patched up, sitting in their usual places. In a ham-handed stab at revisionist history, the slain dignitaries were replaced by roughly similar looking doppelgangers, robed in the same hokey outfits. The vassals of totalitarian rulers were often coerced to accept a manufactured reality; but was Kaufman also expected to play along, pretending that nothing ever happened?

There was no more string quartet or roast boar, but the domestics still made a valiant effort to keep up appearances. Their lives likely depended on it.

Everyone quietly chewed their food, waiting for dour Makanga to stop brooding and lead the conversation.

"Mr. Kaufman, we are in a very awkward position," he finally admitted. "Please do not think that today's unfortunate, eh, incident is normal for our country. Ours is a land of peace and prosperity, with different ethnic groups living in harmony..."

"Mr. President," Kaufman cut him off. He was rattled, and out of patience for platitudes. "Who are those children?"

Makanga was taken aback for a moment, strategizing how best to answer. People kept deviating from the script he had prepared for Kaufman's visit – first his choreographed mine tour was a bloody catastrophe and now the insolent analyst wasn't even sitting through the general's monolog.

"They are just criminals," Makanga dismissed the question.

"But what did they want?"

"Clearly, they wanted to steal the coltan." The dictator's annoyance was visibly mounting. He hadn't answered to anyone in years.

"Then why would they attack from the other side of the river? They couldn't possibly swim across and take the barrels back with them. It looks like they just wanted to kill you."

Makanga's first instinct was to draw his weapon and ventilate Kaufman's face. But he restrained himself. The general desperately needed backing and even *he* couldn't survive the wrath of Milos Sterling.

Makanga fumed for a few tense seconds. The luminaries quivered and perspired. They were actually more frightened at this instant than they were in the day's gory ambush. If Makanga slid into one of his dreaded tantrums, in this confined space, no one would make it out alive.

"Those children are demons," Makanga stammered.

"What's their issue? I mean, what's their point of view?" Kaufman was emboldened, having already flirted so closely with death.

Makanga dropped his silverware in an impotent show of exasperation. The dignitaries slouched lower in their chairs, wishing they could just disappear.

"How can I know their point of view?!" Makanga roared. "They are hateful little animals with no desire for civilization. They don't have a point of view."

The sycophants were visibly trembling.

"Who gave them the guns?"

"My enemies."

Kaufman shook his head in disbelief. Did Makanga think he could actually give him the runaround? The Jupiter Fund did not make opaque investments. Kaufman sucked in air, about to launch into a tirade, when he saw something genuinely terrifying flare up in Makanga's eyes. Kaufman now fully realized he was on thin ice. He resolved to shut his big mouth.

Makanga abruptly waved his hand, as if to conclude the discussion. "Mr. Kaufman, this is none of your concern. I can assure you that the threat to the mining operation will soon be eliminated and full output shall resume. You will stay here a few more days, and you will see that our mine is an excellent investment." With staggering effort, Makanga forced a smile. The dignitaries all nodded in vigorous agreement, their eyes pleading with Kaufman to take the hint.

Kaufman fixated on the general's phrasing. He will stay a few more days? Did Makanga really mean to say that Kaufman had no choice?

After hours of tossing and turning, Kaufman gave up on the prospect of sleep. He was beyond the point of exhaustion – his eyes bugged out of their sockets, but his survival instinct kept his nervous system tingling on high alert.

He paced back and forth in his underwear, talking to Milos on a gilded telephone.

"Milos, this is getting way too heavy. Whatever you think you stand to make, I can assure you it's not worth it."

"What's the problem?" Milos sounded oblivious.

"I don't think you're hearing me," Kaufman blustered.

"No Kaufman, I'm hearing you. I don't think you're hearing me," Milos sounded wary. "Please, be careful."

"What do you know that I don't?" Kaufman hissed.

"Kaufman, *please be careful*," Milos repeated. He was clearly holding something back. Kaufman realized he was being indiscreet on an insecure line. Circumstances had clouded his judgment.

Kaufman peered out the window and saw the compound was reinforced with more armed sentries, patrolling the perimeter. He fell silent.

"Kaufman? Are you there? What's going on?"

Kaufman heard a click and a little more static on the line. He looked askance at the receiver, his fears confirmed.

"Hey, let me call you back later, okay?" Kaufman hung up without waiting for a response.

A couple hours before daybreak, Kaufman still lay in bed with eyes wide open, his head swimming with anxiety. He wished he could go to sleep and leave this ugly place for a while.

Makanga suddenly barged through the door in his pajamas and a leopard fur robe. Kaufman bolted upright in alarm. Makanga pulled up a chair next to his bed, as if this were perfectly normal behavior. Kaufman blinked in panicked disbelief.

"Sorry to disturb your rest. I myself have also been unable to sleep." Makanga was so unnervingly close. Kaufman could see the tiny muscles twitching in his face and smell his sour night breath.

Kaufman opened his mouth, but words did not come out. He realized Makanga could strangle him with his beastly hands and no one would hear a sound.

"I feel you do not trust me." Makanga waited for some kind of reassurance, but none was forthcoming.

"Perhaps you don't understand me. I was born in the mud. With nothing. And I clawed my way to this station in life... I do love my people. And that is why I must be so hard on them. This land is wild. There is no order unless it is enforced with an iron fist." Makanga scrutinized his houseguest, who was still petrified and slack-jawed. "Kaufman, please tell me about yourself."

Kaufman finally managed to force out some words: "General, could we maybe talk lat..."

"I know a few things about you," Makanga interrupted. "You are twenty-eight years old. Your parents, Maude and Edward, live in Brookfield, New Hampshire. You volunteer at the

Garcia Youth Center, three miles and worlds away from your fancy apartment."

Kaufman's throat constricted.

"Your coworkers don't know that, do they?" Makanga's tone grew ominous. "But I do. I am a man of means. And my influence extends well beyond the confines of this modest land. I am very good to my friends and merciless to my enemies... I hope we can be friends."

"I don't make any decisions," Kaufman blurted.

"I know. But this deal is very important to me, and I need an ally to make it work. I am very good to my allies."

Makanga stood and sauntered out the door, affecting casual ease.

Kaufman clenched his jaw and broke into heaving hyper-ventilation. He heard the distant, muffled scream of someone tortured in another room. Kaufman snapped. He leapt out of bed and haphazardly threw on his clothes.

Kaufman darted into the hallway, only to be barricaded by a towering guard holding a submachine gun. The man's eyes were vacant and unblinking.

Kaufman stared him down for a second, but there was no reaction. He tried to skirt around the mountain of a man, but the guard raised his hand to halt him.

"Mr. Kaufman, I have been told to guard your room," he droned.

"Okay, guard it." Kaufman tried again to slip past him.

"Please, you will be much safer inside. And there is a guided tour scheduled for you bright and early tomorrow morning." It seemed like the brute was struggling to remember his lines. He flashed a plastic smile, but his eyes were still blank. Kaufman nervously glanced at the machine gun, then retreated back into his room.

He paced back and forth again, his mind clouded in survival mode, struggling to assess his options. Under the general's roof, he was subject to Makanga's total dominion, existing entirely at his mercy. He had no free will and his fate was out of his hands. But he also had no clue what dangers lurked in the black void outside the compound.

Kaufman snatched his passport and wallet, slipped out the window and climbed the wall. He reached the roof and crawled across the slanted ridge, slithering through shadows so he wouldn't be spotted by guards.

A shingle gave out under his hand, and he tumbled down the incline. His heart hammered – soon he would be free-falling off the side of the palace to meet an ignominious end, snapping his neck against the earth. But he managed to catch hold of a rain gutter, right at the precipice and weaseled back onto the rooftop.

He crawled to the back of the palace, shimmied down a succession of window moldings, then dropped to the dirt with a thud.

Kaufman crept along the concrete outer wall in darkness, until he found a section with vines growing up the side. He waited until the searchlight passed, then scrambled up the wall and hastily flopped over the top. He hit the ground on the other side and his elbows impacted against his ribs, knocking the wind out of him. Kaufman fled into the shadows, gasping for air.

He wandered the jungle, dirty and lost. He heard eerie animal howls and cringed in mortal fear; but kept pushing deeper and deeper into the darkness – because the beasts in the wild weren't nearly as frightening as the animals in Makanga's employ. Once his last ounce of strength was spent, Kaufman struggled up a tree, in hopes of stealing a moment's rest. Hungry eyes watched him as he dozed.

20

Smiling theatrically and carrying a tray of sticky breakfast foods, Niambi extended her graceful neck into Kaufman's suite.

"Mr. Kaufman, we have some surprises for you!" She saw the bed empty and the window ajar.

The phony smile slid right off her face. She was instantly scheming and scrambling for a way to pin the blame for Kaufman's absence on someone else – perhaps the guards or the servants – anyone to take the fall, because she knew how precipitous it would be. Of course it wasn't her fault, but that would not stop Makanga from lumping her in the pending inquisition.

Filthy Kaufman stumbled out of the jungle, so much worse for wear. He was coated in layers of dirt, sap, sweat and swollen, oozing insect bites. He had managed a few minutes of semi-sleep, clinging to rough tree bark, but his eyes were puffy and his head throbbed.

Kaufman found himself at the outskirts of a shanty town. So many shacks were cobbled together from rusty corrugated metal, cracked plywood, plastic tarps and anything else that might put up some slight resistance against the elements. This township was the worst of both worlds – not large enough to provide opportunity, like in a city; but also not small enough to foster community, like in a village. It was just a hopeless slum, where the disaffected poor bickered and fought over crumbs.

Women hanging laundry gave Kaufman the evil eye. Where on earth did this awkward white man come from? What did he want? The likes of Kaufman only showed their faces when they sought to recruit dirt-cheap labor or con them out of mineral rights.

Kaufman trudged through a narrow alleyway and a sweet-faced toddler approached him with curious eyes. Kaufman flashed a world-weary smile. This was the first human being he met in days who wasn't trying to game him. The boy reached out his hand. Kaufman extended his as well, but the child's young mother charged over and yanked him away, in fear of the greasy, white boogeyman. She spat on the ground at Kaufman's feet, shot him a withering look and marched off with her wriggling tot under her arm.

Kaufman stumbled deeper into town, sidestepping raw sewage, dead rodents and soiled undergarments. Several more fonts of putrescence competed to overpower his nose.

He passed some older children battering a soccer ball, throwing elbows and screaming in each other's faces. Even scruffier kids sat on the sidelines with glassy, bloodshot eyes, huffing glue out of paper bags.

A shopkeeper marched onto the porch and barked at them. They waved him off, swamped in their stupor. He swung a broom threateningly, but they just shrugged, listless. The shopkeeper spotted Kaufman, hobbling by like a zombie and retreated into his store – as if Kaufman meant more trouble than the stoned urchins obstructing his business.

Kaufman reached the central strip of dirt that passed for Main Street. A gang of amputees spotted his lily face and practically flew off the curb to mob him with outstretched prosthetics made of coat hangers. Kaufman was encircled by fraught, hungry faces covered in crud and open boils, pleading for any food scrap or centime he could spare. He dug into his pockets, found some crumpled U.S. Dollars and handed them over, as he tried to dodge their claws. A brawl erupted over the cash. They hacked at each other in feral desperation. One man almost had his eye gouged out before he finally relinquished a one dollar bill. Kaufman wriggled free and took refuge in the nearest open shack.

He found himself in the seediest dive in the world. Not one chair matched another. The tables were jerry-rigged particle boards, tagged and carved by generations of vandals. The rusty, patchwork walls were covered in scrawling and long outdated bikini calendars – with grainy photographs of models sporting permed 1980s hair and fluorescent swimsuits. Kaufman may have been coated in grime, but he looked spotless by comparison to the grizzled, shifty characters swilling all manner of cheap sauce. An elephantine bartender sat on a buckling stool, watching mostly static on a black and white television. A few sloshed drunkards played cards on a folding table, slapping down their hands and threatening to strangle each other upon nonpayment. An ancient, painted hooker filed her nails, nursing a cocktail.

Kaufman lurched up to the bar. "Bottled water?"

The barkeep laughed in his face.

"Bottled beer?" Kaufman would settle for any sealed beverage, to reduce the risk of ingesting parasites.

The mammoth barman deigned to heft up and fetch Kaufman a bottle of Primus.

"800 Franc," he mumbled.

Kaufman rifled through his pocket.

"Don't let 'im gyp you, that's four times the going rate."

Kaufman furrowed his brow – did his ears deceive him or was there an Australian inexplicably in his presence? He turned to see a portly, red-faced man blotting out the doorway. He had a curly mop of white hair and crusty sweat stains on his safari shirt. The man waddled over and clapped Kaufman on the back.

"Put it on my tab," the cooked Australian winked at Kaufman. The Bartender sneered and flopped back on his belabored stool.

"Thanks." Kaufman was grateful for his kindness, but he wasn't inclined to trust him. The man didn't exactly look like he was there for humanitarian work.

"Not from these parts, eh?" The girthsome Aussie's breathing was audibly strained.

"No. Are you?"

The man rolled his eyes. "Yeah, I was born in the 'eart of Africa." He extended his sausage-link fingers to shake.

"Jimmy Duncan."

"Kaufman."

Jimmy opened his throat, guzzled his beer, then leaned in for a whisper. "What brings you to this wasteland? Diamonds? Gold? Oil?" Hot beer breath enveloped Kaufman's face.

"I can't really say."

Jimmy unleashed a deep belly laugh.

"Darky pussy?"

Kaufman looked around to see if Jimmy had ruffled any local feathers, but they paid him no mind.

"Yeah, that's it," Kaufman groaned.

Jimmy chortled. "Listen, I got some merchandise to show you."

"I was kidding."

"No, some beautiful rough stones." Jimmy reached into his pocket and produced several bulbous, uncut diamonds – a handful worth more than a house.

"I'm not in the market."

"You ain't even heard my prices!" Jimmy protested.

"I'm not here to buy anything."

"You with the U.N. or something?" Jimmy squinted at Kaufman with suspicion, shoved the rocks back in his pocket.

"No."

Jimmy looked him up and down. "What a queer little kitty!"

Kaufman shrugged. With nothing to gain, Jimmy returned to his beer. Awkward eons passed.

"You know how to get to the airport?" Kaufman whispered, afraid to sound any more like a clueless tourist.

"Sure, let me show you." Jimmy cracked a yellow smile, clutched Kaufman's arm and led him out of the bar. "You just take the Lualaba Expressway north to the..." They barely cleared the doorway, when Jimmy smashed his beer bottle on the back of Kaufman's head. Kaufman collapsed like a sack of garbage. Jimmy snaked his wallet and skirted off into the street. The locals didn't bat an eye.

Day turned to night and people casually stepped over unconscious, drooling Kaufman as they went about their business.

His eyes finally opened to slits and he woozily struggled upright, rubbing his throbbing head. A flash of panic coursed through him as he remembered where he was. Kaufman checked his pockets and found he had been relieved of all possessions. At least he was somehow still breathing. But with no food, friends or resources in this perilous place, he was living on borrowed time.

The streets were desolate during the day, but now they were palpably dangerous. Various rebel factions had emerged from the woodwork. They wore paramilitary uniforms mixed in with civilian clothes. Each had an AK-47 strapped to his (sometimes her) back. Some wore Tupac shirts and listened to boom boxes, some smoked hash, others negotiated aggressively with prostitutes.

Kaufman instantly recognized that disparate, heavily armed gangs, hopped up on various drugs and confined to the same narrow drag, was a powder keg primed to erupt at any moment. And Kaufman was easily expendable – the obvious odd-man-out. He tried to slip into the shadows, but a band of stoned rebels spotted his clumsy sidestep and burst out laughing.

The leader was a muscle-bound teenager with a peach fuzz moustache. "Look a white gorilla – my favorite food!" He giggled to his cronies.

They cracked up as he made a mugging dumb show of shouldering his rifle and tiptoeing over to Kaufman. Kaufman was fossilized in fear. The hoodlum poked Kaufman in the stomach with the barrel of his gun. "Such soft meat!"

The lackeys broke into another round of obsequious laughter, as if everything their leader said was pure, comic gold. Kaufman's stomach did somersaults. Up close, the boy smelled strongly of paint thinner. His nostrils were scabby and inflamed from huffing poison.

"Sorry we gotta kill you, but we hungry as hell." He prodded Kaufman's belly a few more times just to watch him squirm. The flunkies indulged in several more rounds of convulsive laughter. Joints and bottles of hooch were passed around to better enjoy the spectacle. "Maybe if you give us a little gift we won't have to lay you on your back."

Kaufman made a show of frantically searching his pockets, but he knew they were already strip-mined.

"No? Too bad..." The thug raised his weapon and chambered a round.

Kaufman winced. He hadn't had much of an eventful life to flash through his mind. So he spent his last breath cursing Milos for sending him to this hell hole.

A bullet cut through the air and punched into the leader's skull, bursting it like a rotten melon. His lifeless body plopped on the dirt, leaking blood and grey matter on Kaufman's shoes.

Kaufman and the cronies all whipped their heads in the direction of the shot. There Sebu stood with his rifle smoking in his hands and his boys flanking him with weapons aimed.

The gang spun to return fire, but they were wasted in a flurry of bullets, collapsing to the ground like marionettes with cut strings.

Panicked, Kaufman leapt to his feet and sprinted away, his neurons crackling in a storm of confusion and fear. He thought he recognized those boys, but he wasn't sure. Why had they missed him, when their other targets were so efficiently dispatched? Would he soon feel a bullet rip through his heart? Would he even be able to feel the kill shot, or would it just shut him down before he knew what hit him?

Sebu shook his head and gestured in Kaufman's direction.

Five of the smaller children charged after him, leapt on his back and they all collapsed in a dusty dog-pile. A rifle butt cracked against his cranium, and darkness engulfed him again.

21

Kaufman woke up even groggier, his head feeling like it belonged to someone else, his thoughts bubbling up lamely in slow-motion. He looked down to find himself tied to a tree, in the middle of endless jungle. He tried to wriggle free, but the bindings were unyielding. By now Kaufman intimately understood that his fate was not in his hands. He had little energy left in his body to affect a tolerable outcome — at this point it was a matter of damage control. The best strategy he could conceive in a pinch, was to determine what these little hell spawn wanted from him and then to leverage it for his life.

He peered around the child soldiers' camp and saw the kids acting predictably rough and savage with each other — cursing, fighting and smoking hash. But he was also surprised to feel a familial warmth. Older boys cooked, and bandaged up the young ones. Their weapons were still resting ominously within arm's reach, but they were ignored for the moment.

"What is this — Lord of the Flies?" Kaufman mumbled to himself.

Lumumba strutted over with his chest puffed out, trying to look tough.

"Who are you?" Lumumba growled.

"My name is Kaufman." They struggled to understand each other's French — Kaufman's was stilted and academic, while the boys had a Congolese patois he strained to follow.

"What were you doing at the mine?" Lumumba closely scrutinized Kaufman's face, trying to sniff out any lies.

Kaufman's mind scrambled to imagine what the boy wanted to hear. Should he confess that he was there to appraise the mine as an investment? On one hand, that might give them the impression that Kaufman was wealthy enough to hold for ransom, which Milos would surely pay for his safety. On the other hand, if the children had some kind of personal axe to grind, they might be more inclined to summarily execute anyone even tangentially involved in the mining operation. Kaufman wished he knew whether they were fighting for personal gain or for some kind of radical ideology. Such knowledge would certainly color his answer.

"I guess I was looking at it," Kaufman mumbled meekly. His answer came out sounding more like a question.

Lumumba backhanded Kaufman with all his might, drawing blood from his lip, cracking his skull against the tree. Kaufman's strategy wasn't playing out like he imagined.

"Don't be smart with me," Lumumba hissed. "Why have you left the comfort of whatever cream puff country you are from? Why are you in this hell? Are you a killer? A banker? A spy?"

"No," Kaufman groaned.

Lumumba kicked him in the chest, evacuating the air from his lungs. He pulled his bayonet and pressed it against Kaufman's throat, drawing a trickle of blood. "Tell me one more lie and I swear you'll regret it." Lumumba whispered his homicidal vow softly into his ear.

Kaufman's diaphragm heaved and jerked, unable to re-inflate his lungs.

Sebu emerged from the shadows to call Lumumba off. He crouched to face Kaufman eye to eye, carefully studying his face. He could sense Kaufman was so far out of his depth. He glanced at his soft hands and knew he had lived a sheltered life. "He is not a warrior. That much is clear."

Kaufman gasped in relief, desperately sucking back oxygen.

"What are you doing here?" Sebu looked quizzically into Kaufman's eyes.

"Believe me, I wish I were anywhere else. I was sent by an American company to study the mine." He gave up on the prospect of spinning the truth. All his fancy, Ivy League game theory and negotiating tactics imploded under the slightest duress.

"Another bloody foreigner has come to rape our land!" Lumumba erupted.

Kaufman hesitated again – the wrong response could get his jaw broken or a knife jammed in his guts. The tall boy seemed like a psychopath. Kaufman just prayed the shorter one would continue protecting him. "We aren't taking anything," Kaufman reasoned, in a measured, humble voice. "We buy your resources – but it's your warlords who sell them to us. They're the ones hacking everyone to pieces."

Lumumba sprung at Kaufman's throat, but Sebu got between them.

"This is half true," Sebu admitted.

"What's the other half?" Kaufman wanted to get him talking, to figure out who these children were and what they wanted.

"Your 'companies' are paying for the killing."

After a moment of reflection, Kaufman grudgingly nodded.

"General Makanga is just another thief."

"So I gathered."

"Will your company buy our stolen earth?"

"I doubt it. Seems like much more trouble than it's worth." Kaufman gestured with his chin to the camp of child soldiers and their automatic weapons. Sebu allowed himself a little laugh.

"We cannot let you go. You know our location." Sebu sounded almost apologetic.

"Oh well, then I guess I'll just rest by this tree."

Kaufman made a cautious joke, pretending to fall back asleep against the trunk. Sebu smiled. Lumumba was hardly won over.

Makanga hunted with his lackeys at dawn. They spent the expedition jockeying for position behind him, lest his frustration boil over and they get a face full of buckshot. The warlord was starting to cave under pressure. His demands of his minions had grown ever more arbitrary and irrational. He seemed to expect the servants to read his mind and bring him things he never actually requested. Perhaps he just wanted any excuse to beat them. Violence was the only thing that temporarily vented his stress.

Milos had already rung the estate a couple times and the servants were running out of explanations for the whiz kid's absence.

The general hastily fired his rifle at a warthog and missed. The report echoed through the jungle and the beast ran for dear life, oinking desperately until he could no longer be heard in the distance. Makanga irritably pulled the bolt and ejected his spent cartridge as a mercenary sidled up with sunken eyes.

"Where is he?" Makanga growled.

"We haven't found him yet, sir," the soldier truckled. "But we will. We will scour the whole jungle if need be."

"Good. Your life depends on it."

The man bowed slightly and hustled off in dread.

Kaufman awoke to Sebu hacking the ropes that bound him.

"You will need your energy." He handed Kaufman a bowl of gruel. Kaufman rubbed his eyes and looked around. The sun was still just a sliver on the horizon as the boys scrambled to gobble their breakfast, gather their belongings and load their weapons. He realized they were remarkably disciplined and well trained. When Kaufman was their age, his mother still made him peanut butter sandwiches and he spent his days in suburban indolence, reading in public libraries and tinkering with computers.

The children marched in a column through miles of copious flora. Sebu blazed a trail with his machete. Lumumba pushed Kaufman along in the rear.

They heard a faint howl, far away.

"Mai-Mai?!" Innocent panicked.

The tiny boy's proclamation sent a shockwave through the ranks. Kaufman was perplexed to see them break into fearful speculation. The boys trembled and perspired. They appeared to be more fearful of this mysterious "Mai-Mai" than they were of Makanga and his entire army. Was it some sort of pagan religious fable that haunted their nightmares? Perhaps "Mai-Mai" was a mythical boogeyman hiding in the jungle?

"*Shhhhhh.*" Sebu listened carefully for a moment. They heard the howl again, even fainter this time. It sounded vaguely like an animal. "It is not Mai-Mai." The boys slackened in relief and resumed their march.

They reached a well-worn trail and Sebu threw up a fist. The children halted. Sebu pointed his index finger skyward and the boys took it as a signal to sling their rifles and climb.

Kaufman was bewildered. Did they also expect him to ascend a stupid tree? What game were they playing? Lumumba prodded him with his rifle. "Up."

Kaufman grudgingly complied.

The boys waited aloft for hours, silently surveying the land below and communicating with hand signals.

Sebu was perched dangerously low, hanging right over the trail. Kaufman sat on a thick branch next to Lumumba. He was grateful for every chirping bird and cracking twig to break the silence. He finally couldn't take it any longer.

"Is someone actually coming?" Kaufman yawned.

"Shhhhhhhh!" Lumumba shot him the dirtiest look.

"Sorry," Kaufman exclaimed at full volume, almost mocking. He would no longer play this tedious game.

Lumumba handled his bayonet. "Make another sound and I'll cut your throat," he hissed.

Hours later, the sun began to set. They were all hungry, irritable and bored. The older children passed the time making lewd gestures at each other, demonstrating what they would do if they could get their hands on any sort of willing female.

"I have to piss," Kaufman groaned at Lumumba.

"I'm not your babysitter." Lumumba rolled his eyes and pantomimed for Kaufman to urinate from the tree.

Kaufman stood up on his branch and turned away from them in modesty. He sighed as he finally relieved himself, but Lumumba hushed him in mid-stream.

"Seriously?" Kaufman turned back to see Lumumba staring daggers. He spotted what they had been waiting for all these hours, then painfully halted his business and zipped up.

A band of broken villagers were slave-driven at gunpoint, hefting heavy sacks like mules, coated in coltan dust and panting in dehydration. They were shoved down the path by Makanga's muscle-bound goons. The wobbly-kneed slaves were on the verge of collapse under the weight of their burdens. At any sign of falter, the guards rammed them forward with rifle butts and taunted them, taking large, demonstrative gulps from their canteens.

One mercenary's eyes wandered upward. Sebu noticed and shouldered his rifle. The child soldiers held their breaths. The closer the mercenaries came without spotting them, the less likely it would be for them to escape the ambush.

The absent-eyed mercenary spotted Sebu and gasped. Sebu shot his face off.

The mercs panicked and the jungle erupted in a desperate firefight.

Unarmed Kaufman cowered behind his trunk as the mercenaries and child soldiers exchanged shots. The children had greater numbers, the element of surprise, higher ground and some cover in the trees. They felled a couple mercenaries before they even knew what was happening.

The mercs grabbed their prisoners and used them as shields. The kids hesitated and a couple of Sebu's friends were shot out of their lofted positions, their lifeless bodies thudding against hard-packed earth.

Dead-eye Sebu had to be bold, sniping mercenaries and barely missing the captured comrades. The children triangulated their fire and soon they routed their enemies.

The last living mercenary dropped his rifle, threw up his arms and screamed for mercy. Several boys on lower-hanging branches swung down to surround him, shoving their hot barrels in his face.

The others carefully descended to tend to their dead and wounded, to unbind the captured villagers and to harvest the enemies' weapons and supplies. Innocent pulled a pair of combat boots off a fallen mercenary and slipped his tiny feet inside.

Kaufman was still gaping and gasping in his tree, hugging the trunk and hyperventilating. Everything happened so fast. He had felt flurries of air from several of the rounds whizzing by his head. The border between life and death was a matter of millimeters.

Sebu opened one of the bags and nodded with satisfaction – it was packed with coltan. He turned to the prisoner, who was restrained by the boys.

"You killed everything I loved," he screamed in the warrior's ear.

"I'm just a tool," The man pleaded.

Sebu couldn't accept his excuse. He knew it wasn't true. He knew the man would kill him for fun if he had the chance. He pummeled the mercenary with his pistol, looking him right in the eye as he battered his face into mush. He could almost see Makanga's face in his face.

Kaufman stared, stunned by Sebu's explosion, slack-jawed in horror. He still couldn't wrap his mind around him. One minute he was thoughtful and empathic, another he was a stoic leader, now he erupted in pure, animalistic rage. Kaufman guessed the boy was somewhere around fifteen years old. What could have happened to make him this way?

Sebu eventually tired out and let the man's lifeless body collapse on the trail. His gaze met Kaufman's and he saw disgust in his eyes. Sebu felt a flash of shame, but he quickly extinguished it. He knew this soft, white foreigner had not seen what he had seen. He would never understand.

22

Kaufman sulked at the edge of camp, his eyes vacant. Some of the boys stifled tears, others tossed and turned through nightmares. A few took refuge in hash and hooch, self-medicating in a vain attempt to forget that two of their brothers were not coming back.

Kaufman eyed Sebu in the distance, haggling desperately with a pair of shifty coltan dealers. The boys had paid so dearly for the ore – they had better get something meaningful out of it. The middlemen forked over some crumpled bills and a couple boxes of ammunition, then carried the bounty of coltan into the darkness – to shuttle it west, to feed people's swelling hunger for gadgets.

Kaufman wondered if Sebu had naively expected to incur zero casualties in the ambush. Would he still have ordered the mission if he knew ahead of time that two souls would be lost? Was the whole operation really just for money and ammo, or was it more important to disrupt Makanga's supply lines? Perhaps Sebu felt he had to risk a few lives, including his own, for the good of the whole platoon. Without supplies, they would all starve. Kaufman was grateful he didn't have to perform this grim calculus, with consequences that would haunt him for life. He couldn't begin to fathom how a mere teenager did it.

A twinge of guilt nagged at the back of his mind. To what extent were his own economic activities, performed from the comfort of his air-conditioned office in New York, responsible for conflicts like these? Only now did he fully fathom how he and his co-workers played with people's lives, on his computer, as if they were videogames. With a few keystrokes and mouse clicks, they were able to shuttle massive pools of capital from one investment vehicle to another. What shady characters were they bolstering? Did he have blood on his soft, uncalloused hands?

Sebu pocketed the money and walked over. He sensed Kaufman's judgment radiating at him. "I don't care what you think. We have no food."

Kaufman did not know what to think anymore. Suddenly his principles seemed so grey and relative.

"We are surrounded," Sebu continued. "The rebels are in the east, Makanga is in the west and everyone wants us dead. There is a price on our heads, so we cannot show our faces in the market. We need you to buy the food." Sebu shoved the cash into Kaufman's trembling hands.

Sebu led Kaufman alone, hacking through a backwoods trail that was overgrown with vegetation, since the only villagers who used it no longer walked the earth. Sebu had left the platoon behind to recuperate as best they could. Kaufman trudged after him on autopilot, so confused and overwhelmed he didn't know which way was up.

Sebu felt unburdened for the moment, to let Lumumba tend to all those boys. And he knew there was something he could learn from this alien white man, if he had a chance to speak with him.

"We are almost there."

Kaufman nodded.

"They will try to take advantage. Let me tell you the right prices."

"Is this about money?" Kaufman blurted.

"What?"

"This war. Is it all just about money?"

"My war is for revenge."

"When does it end?"

"When Makanga is dead."

"Then what?"

Sebu had no answer. He pulled a rusty .38 revolver from his pocket.

"You know how to use this?"

"I suppose."

"You should keep it for protection." Sebu handed him the weapon.

Kaufman grasped the gun with a faltering hand. Sebu's rifle dangled by his shoulder strap. Why did Sebu trust him? Kaufman could easily have blasted him in the head and ran for his life. No one back home would ever know he did it.

Every moment Kaufman spent with these toxic children was a moment closer to death. But he gritted his teeth and packed the pistol in the back of his pants.

They hacked their way a little deeper, when Sebu stopped and furrowed his brow. He realized he had lost the last trickle of the trail quite a way back and had unknowingly blazed a new path to nowhere.

Sebu slashed a little deeper, before halting dead in his tracks. He let out a tiny gasp, then froze in terror.

"What now?" Kaufman groaned.

"*Shhhhhhh.*"

Sebu pointed to a ghoulish totem imbedded in the earth. It was carved of dark wood and had the face of a crazed beast, with wild eyes and giant, pointy teeth.

"Mai-Mai," Sebu whispered in a panic.

"What does that even mean?" Kaufman grew tired of the endless stream of emergencies, but the grisly totem gave him a hint that "Mai-Mai" wasn't just a fairy story.

"Run!" Sebu turned to sprint from whence they came and Kaufman reluctantly followed. They heard a distant wail.

"Hide," Sebu gasped, barely audible. He dove under a bush and frantically waved at Kaufman to follow. Kaufman grudgingly played along, and they cowered together in the underbrush.

The trees violently rustled all around them. The sound of footfalls darted back and forth. Demented cackles echoed through the trees. Kaufman now shared Sebu's dread.

The Mai-Mai burst through the jungle from every direction, encircling them and blocking any hope of escape. They were savages with freakish decorations, wearing sink plugs and monkey skulls around their necks, their faces painted for war. Some wielded machetes, some heaved spears; others carried corroded old rifles or sawed-off shotguns. They moved in graceless fits and jerks. All looked sweaty and high.

These men were once indigenous tribesmen who just wanted to be left alone. But after suffering a relentless parade of warlords, government forces and foreign invaders shoving them around, trampling and sullying their pure, ancestral lands, they decided to get theatrical. They marked their territory with macabre spectacles and mercilessly executed anyone who encroached on their homes. Their flamboyance and fearlessness struck terminal terror in all enemies.

Sebu cursed himself for leading them astray. Their heads would probably be left to rot on pikes, to deter future trespassers, and Sebu's friends would have to fend for themselves.

The Mai-Mai chief leapt forth, his body undulating in a threatening dance, his feathered headdress flopping along with his wild, darting movements. He sniffed the air and grimaced, as if he could smell the stench of Sebu and Kaufman's fear.

The Mai-Mai closed in, blades drawn, and chattered amongst themselves in an unrecognized dialect. Their weapons thrust forth in unison, rhythmically lurching closer and closer to the trespassers. Mangled spears and rusty gun barrels soon surrounded Kaufman and Sebu from every angle, only inches from their throats. Sebu reached for his AK, but a grizzled foot pinned it to the earth.

The chief sniffed Sebu up and down and wretched in melodramatic disgust. The chief barked at him in his native tongue. Sebu had no clue what he said, but he got the drift from his gestures.

"We did not mean to come here and we swear we will never come back," Sebu struggled to sound calm and conciliatory.

The chief laughed in Sebu's face, assaulting him with acrid vapors – the stench of tooth decay and rotten fruit fermented in pits. He rubbed his fingers together in the universal gesture for money.

Sebu was paralyzed by indecision. He knew the boys relied on this cash for food. They sacrificed so much for it. Giving it up would be the ultimate betrayal – a veritable death sentence for his brothers. But it seemed the Mai-Mai would get their hands on the cash whether he was dead or alive. In the end it didn't matter – the decision was made for him.

Twenty grubby hands snatched at Sebu and Kaufman all at once, like a tentacled leviathan, tearing their pockets open.

A fearsome Mai-Mai warrior snatched Sebu's assault rifle and bore down on the trigger, triumphantly spraying rounds into the air. Hot shell casings rained down and burned Sebu's face.

Kaufman and Sebu were still ossified in fear and confusion, when the Chief swilled from a large jug and sprayed them head to toe with putrid liquid. That was their final humiliation.

The Mai-Mai made off with the pilfered goods and disappeared into the jungle as quickly as they came.

Kaufman and Sebu checked their pockets. They were picked clean. But the Mai-Mai missed the pistol in the back of Kaufman's pants. He raised it to shoot into the jungle where they retreated, but Sebu pushed down his wrist.

"They're only protecting their home." Sebu hung his head.

23

With grumbling stomachs, the boys moped around the camp. Any shred of fun or horseplay was gone. Even the trees seemed to wilt in sympathy. Lumumba struggled to build a tent with rope and tarp, but his hands were weak from hunger.

Kaufman tried to tighten his belt, but he already used the last hole. He scanned the slouching ranks and felt his heart ache. He had never seen them like this. No matter how deep the boys waded through excrement, their resolve never wavered. Kaufman thought they had an infinite capacity to fight, but now their last shred of hope was snuffed.

Kaufman saw Sebu dejectedly sewing his pockets back together and in a moment of hungry delirium he saw fit to try to lighten the mood:

"What's the point of pockets when you have nothing to put in them?" No one was amused. "You expecting your rich uncle to die?" He kept digging himself deeper. Boys rolled over on the ground so they didn't have to look at his dumb, white face. "Aren't there any animals we could eat?" Kaufman was so hungry he'd eat dirt.

"A gorilla would be nice," Sebu chimed in.

"They're endangered."

"So are we."

The rope snapped in Lumumba's face and his tent caved in. Lumumba snapped as well – kicking and punching the tarp in frustration, tangling with it on the ground, quickly tiring himself out and collapsing in a dejected heap.

"Every time we make progress, it is taken away from us," he cried.

The boys agreed that they would have to do something very wrong if they wanted to survive. For several famished hours, Kaufman sat on a fallen log at the side of a path, drumming absentmindedly with a pair of sticks, waiting for his cue to act.

Hunger and boredom converged on him and he imagined himself drifting up through the dense, green jungle canopy and seeing the whole breathing, teeming ecosystem from the sky. Human beings looked like ants – desperately trying to assert themselves in the vast expanse. But they were at odds; out of synch with the ebb and flow and rhythm of nature. They could build towering monuments to their vanity, but all would eventually crumble and be swallowed back into the earth.

Kaufman finally heard crunching leaves farther down the trail, which snapped him out of his trance. He steeled himself to play his part.

A ragged woman rounded the bend, pushing a sparsely filled fruit cart to market. She stared at Kaufman like he had two heads. What on earth was this bizarre looking man doing on a log in the middle of nowhere? Kaufman saw her careworn face and wished it was anyone but her. He knew they should have conceived a better plan, but their minds were addled by hunger and now it was too late.

"Hi Miss, I wonder if you know where I could find..."

The woman stopped her cart and the children sprung from all around, surrounding her with guns at bay.

She yelped for a second, but her fear was short lived. Her eyes narrowed and she shook her head in disgust.

"Forgive us Mamma, we're very hungry." Sebu reached for her wares. The Woman slapped his wrist. They had chosen the wrong mark. She had clearly faced down far more credible threats, in her decades in such a hostile land.

"Get your dirty hands off my fruit, boy," She bellowed, "You think I'm scared of you because you have a big gun and you think you're a tough guy? You're not. And who is this white devil? A grown man – you should be ashamed of yourself."

Kaufman certainly was. He threw his hands up and skulked off.

"You know what happens if I lose this fruit?" She roared in Sebu's face, unfazed by his weapons. "My own grandchildren go hungry. So if you want it, you might as well just kill me too – you'd be doing me a favor."

"I'm so sorry. Please give us just a little," Sebu begged.

"After you tried to rob me?!"

Off the beaten path, Kaufman shoved through dense vegetation, failing to escape his shame.

His jaw dropped. Mere yards away, a silverback gorilla munched on nettles. He was a massive, majestic creature with thoughtful eyes. Kaufman was close enough to hear him breathe in a low rumble – air resonating through his mighty barrel chest. The gorilla's brow furrowed, which made him look like a wise old man, lost in contemplation. His movements were careful, measured, gentle. He seemed so human. Kaufman wondered what the animal might be thinking. What flashes of intelligence lay behind his deep, black eyes? What visions haunted his dreams?

Kaufman felt an intense rumble in his gut like he never felt before. It was as if a creature lived inside of him, pounding on the walls of his stomach, demanding immediate nourishment. In the distance, he heard the situation with the poor old woman degenerate into pleading and screaming. He knew he had no choice. Kaufman winced, raised his pistol and closed his eyes. "I'm so sorry," he wailed.

Things had gotten uglier back at the path. The woman was irate and Sebu could not appease her.

"Maybe we could just take a couple from the corner and no one would notice?"

The woman filled her lungs for another shrill tirade, when they heard a distant shot.

The boys sat around a roaring bonfire, gleefully devouring bush meat like a starving pack of wolves. The flickering flames cast a golden glow against their faces. Kaufman winced in penance for every bite. He felt himself slipping into tribal atavism, but given the circumstances it felt so natural.

One boy pounded on a makeshift drum he made from a hollow log, while another did a goofy dance for everyone's amusement. A third kid stood to challenge him and they alternated in a competitive dance-off. The children laughed and cheered as they escalated both the intricacy and silliness of their moves.

Finally the first boy collapsed in mock exhaustion, eliciting a hearty round of applause.

Sebu stood and cleared his throat. "Kaufman, we are all thankful for your help today." The children nodded and clapped. Even Lumumba patted Kaufman on the shoulder.

"You're not as rotten as I thought," he conceded.

"That means a lot to me." Kaufman's face betrayed an uncharacteristic hint of emotion.

The drumming started up again and Kaufman tried to fit in, performing an awkward dance.

"You move like a drunken giraffe," one child chided. The boys erupted in mockery.

"More like a pregnant hippo." Another boy imitated Kaufman's clumsy shuffle, which made them all laugh even harder.

Innocent was on lookout duty in a tree. He heard the drumming and mirth in the distance, but it was his turn to sit out the fun. The little boy squinted into the jungle and gasped.

"Help!" He screamed. A bullet tore through his tiny heart and instantly extinguished him. His slight body slammed down on the jungle floor.

The boys around the fire heard heavy boots trampling toward the camp. They scrambled for their guns. The stomping grew louder and closer.

A wave of vicious mercenaries exploded from the jungle and swarmed the camp. The boys scattered, dug their heels and opened fire. They managed to halt the charge and the column of attackers fanned out, with mercenaries taking positions behind the cover of rocks and trees.

The children pitched and rolled, mastering their terrain and dominating their attackers – until the second wave poured in. The reinforcements were far more numerous. They battered the children's positions and blasted apart their flimsy tents.

Kaufman trembled, hiding behind a wide tree trunk, facing away from the firefight.

Sebu was terrified. They had always chosen their battles on their own terms. They relied on the element of surprise. Their strikes were surgical and meticulously planned. But now they were the ones being ambushed. They could never win this way. Would this be their last stand?

"Fall back!" Sebu screamed. They retreated into the jungle, but Sebu stayed back to cover their escape. He sprayed bullets indiscriminately, managing to hold the killers off long enough for all of his brothers to disappear into the darkness.

But then his mag ran out. Sebu's heart sank. This would surely be the end. Everything he had seen and learned, the memories he had collected, the dreams he had, would all be erased. He took a final breath. The mercenaries aimed, but a mangy commander threw up a fist.

"Wait! I want his head." The monster unsheathed a chipped machete and swaggered over to cowering Sebu. He unknowingly walked by Kaufman, who was still gasping behind the tree.

The commander towered over Sebu and raised his blade to cut him down.

With trembling hands, Kaufman pulled his .38 special and blasted the mercenary in the back of the head. Kaufman's lucky shot punched right through the man's brain stem – it might as well have been an off switch. His body slammed onto Sebu.

The attackers opened fire again. Sebu was both pinned and protected by the corpse. Perforated like Swiss cheese, the man's blood spattered all over him.

Kaufman looked down at his own smoking barrel, half in disbelief. Did he really just kill a man?

The mercenaries got brave and sloppy, leaping out of their positions and charging at Sebu. And then Lumumba came to his rescue, darting from the jungle long enough to blast the lead mercenaries and lay a volley of cover fire, so Sebu and Kaufman could dive into the blackness of night.

A few soldiers chased them into the jungle, while the others stayed to raze the camp.

Sebu and Lumumba zigzagged through the trees, clearly familiar with the territory. Kaufman followed as best he could, trailing by a few paces.

A pile of palm fronds erupted, and a small boy popped out of a secret sinkhole. He beckoned them in. They dove into the pit and barely managed to cover the mouth when another wave of mercs trampled into the clearing. They were confused and frustrated, with no clue where the boys went. So they scattered and ran in every direction.

Sebu, Lumumba and Kaufman wiggled into a tight, musty tunnel. It was lit with a single gas-lamp. The other child soldiers were already settled in, tightly lining the walls and sitting cross-legged. Their eyes darted around in fear and agitation. No one made a sound.

The mercenaries tore the camp to shreds, trampling the boys' meager belongings and stomping them into the dirt. Anything useful or life sustaining was destroyed. Even if they failed to kill the fugitive children, they would still deprive them of their supplies and cripple them any way they could. They mutilated their fallen brothers' bodies out of spite. If they couldn't slaughter every child outright, they would do anything in their power to crush their spirits and annihilate whatever source of comfort or refuge they might have.

Kaufman and the boys spent the night catching cramped catnaps, unable to stretch any appendage, ever vigilant for the sound of heavy boots.

At sunrise, Sebu peeked out and filled his lungs with fresh air. Once he was satisfied that the grim reapers were gone, he beckoned everyone to the surface.

Kaufman and the children poked around the scorched ruins of their camp. They found their brothers' bodies torn asunder, strewn about the dirt. A young boy dropped to his knees and cried.

They had nothing left but guns and hate.

Lumumba pounded his fists into a tree trunk until they bled. Sebu sat on the ground hugging his knees and rocking like the child he really was.

Kaufman looked at the dead children and his sight went red. His stomach swirled with nausea, his head throbbed with rage. The last remnants of his sanitized self, of his detached erudition, of his caution and timidity were gone. He couldn't comprehend the sickness of this place. There was no intellectual answer – it was all visceral. He wanted to snap someone's neck. He wanted to crush every bone in Makanga's body and bury him alive.

"This will end," Kaufman vowed. He charged over to Sebu's pack and took out his map. He held it up to Lumumba. "You have one too?"

Bewildered Lumumba nodded.

Kaufman stomped off into the jungle in the direction from which the mercenaries came.

"You are leaving us?" Sebu called out after him, feeling so betrayed. Kaufman didn't hear the question – he was already gone.

24

Kaufman tore through the jungle, barreling over the flora with singular drive. His mind no longer drifted like a cloud of curiosity. It was focused, wielded like a hammer that would batter through resistance and force what was right. He panted and huffed and sweated through his shirt.

He jammed through the shantytown and this time no one stared. They didn't see a victim, or a tourist, or a lost soul – they saw a man with purpose. He was prepared to blast past anyone who stood in his way.

Kaufman flailed, drenched and breathless, into a hard landing at Makanga's outer gate. He banged on the guardhouse window. One guard's face stayed buried in a porn magazine, while the other looked up in irritation.

"I must speak with Makanga," Kaufman demanded.

The first guard laughed in his face. "The President is not here today."

"Where can I find him?"

The guard turned to his colleague, bemused at Kaufman's nerve. "Who is this boy?"

The Second Guard pried his eyes up from his smut and they bulged in recognition. He dropped his magazine, rushed out of the booth and grabbed Kaufman firmly by the forearm.

"Mr. Kaufman, it is so good to see you. Please come with me." He cracked an unctuous smile and dragged him through the gate into the palace grounds. Kaufman finally registered alarm. Perhaps he should have thought his plan through a little better.

The guard shoved Kaufman though the ornate entrance and everyone halted their work to gape for a moment. It was like some mythical creature had finally been captured – they were taking the elusive Sasquatch in for questioning. Makanga's minions were all so relieved to have him back in custody, since his absence sparked a reign of terror. The General took his frustration out on all of them – from the highest ranking commander to the lowliest chamber maid.

More troops blocked the front door behind Kaufman, cutting off any potential for escape. His self-preservation instinct finally returned to him and he spoke with a shred of humility. "May I please speak to Makanga?"

The guard shoved Kaufman against a wall to forcefully manhandle and frisk him for weapons. The soldier gasped when he found the rusty revolver in Kaufman's pants, then barked some kind of alarm.

"No, I just want to talk!" Kaufman pleaded, realizing how bad it looked.

More guards rushed over in a panic. One knocked him out with a punch to jaw, as the others dog-piled and cuffed him on the ground.

A bucket of rancid water splashed in Kaufman's face, jolting him awake. It stung the growing, purple welt left by the soldier's meaty fist. He shivered as it soaked his shirt and trickled down his body. Now he smelled worse than a rotting wildebeest.

He found himself cuffed at the wrists and ankles, in a pain position on a hard metal stool. He was unable to sit upright or stretch his legs at all. His neck was already stiff and throbbing. How long was he out?

Kaufman tried to look around, but he was completely submerged in darkness. The room was dead silent.

"Hello?" His voice did not reverberate at all – it was swallowed by the walls. Kaufman gathered that the space was small and lined with foam noise padding. They could cut his head off with a butter knife, and no one would hear him scream.

A monstrous minotaur of a man emerged from the shadows, sporting a wide, Cheshire grin, while his beady eyes glared contemptuously at Kaufman. Muscles rippled and bulged through his suit.

"So kind of you to join me," the interrogator taunted.

Kaufman tried to make out his face, but the light was so harsh and glaring that all he could see was the interrogator's beady, ferret eyes.

"Who do you work for?" The man sounded suave and pleasant, with a deep timbre in his voice.

"The Jupiter Fund," Kaufman murmured.

The interrogator slammed Kaufman's revolver on the table, startling Kaufman in his seat. He jerked upright and pulled a muscle in his restrained shoulder. But he was relieved that the faulty weapon didn't accidentally discharge.

"Since when do hedge funds arm their analysts? Are you CIA? MI6? Mossad? Don't try my patience, boy." The interrogator shoved the pistol in Kaufman's face and thumbed back the hammer.

"What kind of retarded operative barges loudly through the front door, packing a Saturday night special?"

The ogre pistol-whipped Kaufman across the face, gashing his cheek and drawing blood. "You tell me."

"I didn't realize I still had it," Kaufman groaned. Kaufman's mind scrambled to determine the optimal story to tell the brute, but he kept arriving at the same conclusion – all answers were wrong answers.

The interrogator shoved the snub barrel in Kaufman's mouth. "Why did you have the weapon in the first place?"

Kaufman searched for an acceptable answer. His eyes darted up and left. The giant recognized this as a very amateur tell – Kaufman's mind was constructing a lie. The interrogator pulled the trigger. Kaufman's eyes bugged and he issued a muffled scream.

Click.

"I won't let you off so easy." The hulk stood and walked to a cabinet, opened a drawer and slipped on latex gloves. "First I must have my fun." He laid out a kit of various barbed instruments. They were all razor sharp and mirror-polished like surgical tools – but none could have served any practical purpose, except to inflict pain. Perhaps they were inspired by mediaeval torture implements or the trappings of the Spanish Inquisition.

"Now I suggest you answer every question in a timely and direct manner." He lifted the smallest, least threatening implement at first, and held it up for Kaufman to see. It was a like miniature version of Poseidon's trident. Given the circumstances, the cuteness was lost on Kaufman. The interrogator smiled with psychotic glee. This was clearly his favorite part of the job.

"Why did you disappear and where did you go?" The fiend asked with more feigned politeness.

"This really isn't necessary. I'm not keeping any secrets."

The interrogator jabbed Kaufman in the hand, making him scream. Blood gushed out of his small, deep wound like a fountain – the man knew how to hit an artery with surgical precision. "I told you to answer every question in a timely and direct manner." He fetched a slightly nastier tool – like a meat tenderizing hammer with extra sharp teeth. Kaufman clenched his jaw and tried to press his wound with his other chained hand.

"As I was saying..." The interrogator held his new toy up to Kaufman's dilated eye.

The door opened, and Makanga sauntered in, flanked by bodyguards. He smiled magnanimously and spitefully at the same time.

"That is enough. We sorted everything out. He is not an assassin or a spy. Just a boy who has grown, as they say, 'too big for his britches.' His employer has requested his immediate return."

Kaufman exhaled in deep relief – he didn't think he'd make it out of the room alive. The inquisitor clenched his fists in frustration.

"Mr. Makanga..." Kaufman fidgeted, still unable to straighten his neck or look him in the eye.

"President Makanga," the warlord corrected.

"President Makanga, I must speak to you."

"What happened to your hand? *Sporting accident?*" Makanga menaced.

"Sure," Kaufman sighed.

"There is no time to sit and chat. I promised to personally see you board the next plane to New York. You may speak to me on the way to the airport."

Kaufman fidgeted in the back of Makanga's second armored limousine, again accompanied by the whole pompous convoy. He was back to sitting uncomfortably close to the general, still lorded over by thuggish guards.

Kaufman gathered his thoughts, trying to wind down from his recent panic so he could negotiate in earnest. Makanga scrawled a long number on a vellum card and handed it to Kaufman. He studied the card for a moment, then rolled his eyes.

"Let me guess – a numbered Swiss account to be filled with millions of dollars if I smooth over the deal?"

"You're smarter than you act."

"I don't want your money." Kaufman flicked the card back at Makanga's face, which made his blood boil. The guards instinctively reached into their coats for their .45 hand cannons, but Makanga waved them off. Kaufman instantly regretted his rashness, but he couldn't help himself. After what he had seen, he could no longer feign respect for the warlord.

"What do you want?" Makanga sighed, patronizing; as if trying to placate an unreasonable child.

"I cannot speak for my firm. The decision isn't mine."

"Granted. But what do you *want*?"

"Amnesty. For the children."

Makanga sat stone faced for a moment, plotting his next move. What was he willing to admit?

"I'm only asking you to stop killing them," Kaufman implored.

"They tried to kill me."

"We can work something out."

Makanga laughed. "Why are you so concerned with these murderers? Because they are children? You know they are guilty of the most hideous crimes? They were more ruthless than adults – they raped, they murdered, they mutilated bodies to make examples of them."

Kaufman winced in hesitation. Could any of this be true? He barely knew the children, but it didn't sound like them. Although he did see Sebu's primal rage unleashed on the captured soldier. "Please stop the car." Kaufman needed space to think.

Makanga shook his head. "I promised to have you on that plane."

"Just stop it for a minute," Kaufman pleaded.

Makanga laughed in his face. "Young man, I'm doing this for your own good. My savage land does not agree with your delicate constitution. You won't survive here. You are far better off in the comfort and safety of your soft United States."

Kaufman pantomimed grudging acceptance. His eyes darted around for an opportunity. A few awkward moments later, the car slowed to round a corner. Kaufman flung the door open and leapt out, rolling in the dirt to disperse his momentum, like he had seen in action movies.

It took a few seconds for the convoy to screech to a halt. They had to begin braking from the rear vehicle to avoid a pileup. Kaufman got a few second head start.

"Bring him back!" Makanga roared.

The guards leapt out and chased Kaufman into an open air market. Makanga shook his head. "He's far more trouble than he's worth."

Kaufman floundered through a bustling bazaar, past villagers who sold fruits, meats and spices. He pushed and weaved around the crowd, with Makanga's goons hot on his tail.

"Try my sweet bananas!" A merchant attempted to slow him down to sample his wares. Kaufman shot by and rounded a corner. The merchant saw the henchmen following and stood in their way as well. "Bananas for the tough guys!"

They too ignored the vendor and dashed deeper into the throng.

Around the corner, Kaufman spotted a small stand filled with dyed fabrics. He dove behind the sheets to hide. The fabric lady shot him a dirty look. "Shoo out of there!"

Kaufman flashed pleading eyes and put his finger to his mouth.

A second later, the guards ran past, but backtracked to question her. "You see a white boy?"

Kaufman shuddered. He was certain she would give him up. She had no incentive to risk her life for a pushy foreigner.

The woman concealed a sneer and pointed the goons in the wrong direction. They ran off in a huff.

"Thank you!" Kaufman peeked out of hiding to express deep gratitude.

"My pleasure. They work for *the bastard*."

25

Ragged Kaufman found his way back to the ruins of the decimated camp. The dead children were buried in neatly dug graves, with lovingly handcrafted markers. The mercenaries were left to rot. Most of their tissue had already been consumed by animals, insects, bacteria and mold. The demon-men had spent their lives destroying and devouring everything around them. Only in death would they foster growth and nourish something other than themselves.

The sight of decaying human beings no longer shocked Kaufman. He was slowly coming to accept that conflict and death was integral to human life, just as it was to animals. He had lived in the sterile fantasyland of the West, where as soon as a person expired he was whisked out of sight, so the indignity of his inanimate body would not upset people's precious sensibilities. They did not even kill their own meat anymore, but outsourced the grisly task to factories that converted breathing creatures into packaged foods that bore little resemblance to the feeling animals from which they were derived.

Kaufman sifted through the wreckage, but found no living souls.

"Sebu? Sebu!" He called out, hearing no answer but the echo of his own voice. He made his way to the hidden tunnel. Kaufman peered into the darkness.

"Sebu?" He groped around until he found the lantern. In the kerosene glow, he saw a scrap of wood with the words "GO TO ULINDI" sloppily carved in.

Kaufman followed his tattered map through backwoods paths, around malarial water holes, skirting past the crudely built fortresses of various rebel factions, slogging across the vast, failed state.

Dripping like a wet rag, he eventually reached Ulindi village square. He lifted his face up from the map to see Sebu and his band of brothers had gathered an angry, scraggly crowd around a makeshift stage of crates and boxes. They held their rifles aloft in the fashion of a militant rally. It seemed everyone was getting into the rhetoric and propaganda game.

"We cannot prosper under Makanga. We cannot let ourselves be enslaved by a criminal who has taken everything from us. Makanga must die!" The crowd roared. Sebu was growing into a charismatic leader.

A browbeaten man threw up his fist. "Death to Makanga!" He shrieked. The villagers joined in, chanting and frothing with rage. In unison, they demanded the warlord's death – each individual synchronizing his thoughts and will with those of the swelling mob.

Sebu spotted Kaufman, smiled and nodded at him. Kaufman pushed his way to the front of the crowd. As usual, people gave him mystified looks.

"Join our rebellion, my brothers and sisters. Together, we can take back our land!" Sebu pumped his rifle in the air. The horde broke into forceful applause. Sebu stomped his feet like a barnstorming preacher. His boys fired celebratory shots into the air.

Kaufman shook his head, knowing this wouldn't end well. These people had drunk the Kool-Aid. They tilted past reason. Their fervor would get them killed. The only hope they had to defeat their oppressor was through rational, methodical planning and application of surgical force. Even then, it was a crap-shoot. What they really needed was for international peacekeepers to intervene. But instead they were raring to charge like idiots and feed themselves to Makanga's insatiable guns.

"And once the blood is spilled and you have control, what will you do with it?" Kaufman was reluctant to speak up, but he felt compelled to sober them with logic. Sebu glared – why was his friend pissing on his parade? The crowd turned on Kaufman, ready to smother him, to confiscate his air so he could no longer spew such impudent drivel. Kaufman was terrified by the fury in their eyes.

"I do not want control," Sebu insisted.

"Then who will take it?" Kaufman forced himself to push through his fear. The truth was too important.

"We can elect a fair leader."

"Think it'll actually happen? Or will you replace one tyrant with another?"

"Who are you to speak to us like this?" The same browbeaten man exploded at Kaufman. He shoved through the crowd with fists clenched, eyes red with anger, itching to clean his clock. Kaufman dodged his first swing.

"Please stop! He is my friend. I will deal with him," Sebu pleaded. The man grudgingly deferred to him. Kaufman let out a world-weary sigh.

Later at night, Sebu glared at Kaufman across a wobbly table, in a borrowed shanty. Lantern light lapped against his eye sockets, only making him look angrier.

"You shouldn't show your face in public," Kaufman urged, ignoring Sebu's ire. He felt an almost paternal duty to speak his mind, even if it strained their friendship.

"These villagers are my allies."

"It only takes one snitch."

Sebu slammed his fist on the table. "Why did you undermine me like that in front of everyone? I should have let them tear you apart." Sebu vented his rage at Kaufman, but once it was spent, he saw his friend look so hurt. Guilt washed over him. He knew Kaufman didn't need to be there. He meant well, even if he didn't understand.

"I've seen enough lives wasted over nothing. It's time to end it," Kaufman implored.

"It will end with Makanga's death." Sebu would not relent. His only reason to exist was to slay the tyrant.

"You're too smart to believe that. It will never end. When he wants a bigger army and more guns, all he has to do is write a check. He can buy all the weapons he needs to wipe you off the earth. And even if you managed to take him out, someone just as bad would replace him." Kaufman's voice cracked with emotion.

"I have no choice," Sebu whispered somberly, though the gravity of Kaufman's words began to sink in.

"Let me try to broker a deal, or find a peacekeeping force."

"It is too late." Sebu knew these were delusions.

"At least let me try."

"Why are you still in this hell-hole? None of this is your problem."

"I don't know. But I'm here. Listen – just disappear for a few days. Don't make any speeches or draw attention to yourself and let me see what I can do. I'll meet you in a week."

Sebu shook his head.

"Please!"

"I don't have a week. They will have hunted us all by then. Maybe I can buy five days."

"Then I'll be back in five days."

26

Kaufman grasped that he was in the eye of a vortex of insanity and his only hope was to appeal to the outside world. Sadly, the outside world didn't care. He knew plenty of people with the leverage to intervene, but they were all preoccupied with other things – like golf handicaps, cosmetic surgery and jet fuel surcharges.

He had to borrow what few measly francs his little friend had, to catch the Ulindi River ferry; which would continue on the Lualaba River, which flowed into the mighty Congo. The Congo River wound like a snake and rushed with unyielding force all the way to Kinshasa. It provided succor to so many – from fish, to hydroelectric power, to transportation through several countries on the sprawling continent. The river was a road.

The barge drifted leisurely at first and the other passengers did not share Kaufman's urgency. In fact, they were all quite content – insulated from their terrestrial squabbles and relatively safe from the deadly crackle of Kalashnikovs. A self-contained economy thrived on deck. Live chickens clucked and wandered freely – their eggs and their bodies were up for sale and consumption. For the right price, the owner would simply pull one up by the legs, snap its neck and remit fresh meat to the buyer. Plucking, dressing and boiling services cost extra.

Two women competed for customers to buy their manioc. They staked their claims to opposite ends of the vessel, pushing their boiled cassava like drug dealers, maligning each other's products and undercutting each other's prices to the brink of mutually assured bankruptcy.

Kaufman had nothing better to do for a while, so he advised them to merge their operations, or at least collude to raise prices to their mutual benefit and to the detriment of their customers. But once the cartel had grown too powerful, the consumers organized a boycott, until Kaufman broke the stalemate and brokered a mutually acceptable, fixed price. He realized he was acting like the Jupiter Fund in miniature, meddling in other people's markets and making casual, thoughtless forays that disproportionately impacted their lives.

Kaufman had not forgotten his mission, but the trip was long and tedious and there was nothing he could do to speed it up. His fellow travelers treated him as an amusing curiosity, touching his hair and peppering him with questions about the Western world.

The boat finally coasted into its destination and Kaufman leapt off the stern. He slammed on the rickety dock and sprinted off to make up for lost time, leaving his fellow voyagers scratching their heads.

He reached a decaying, clapboard corner market on the outskirts of Kinshasa. The shelves were filled with dusty, off-brand canned goods and counterfeit bottles of Coca-Cola. More importantly, it had a payphone and a Western Union terminal. He collect-called his boss.

"...Listen Milos, I'm sorry, I can't leave yet. People will die."

"You don't actually believe you can save them?" Sterling sounded exasperated.

"Probably not. But I have to try."

Milos was silent at the other end. Kaufman heard a raucous

party in the background. He discerned the distinctly affected ban-
ter of Upper Manhattan socialites.

"Look, I still haven't used my vacation days."

"Kaufman, you're being stupid."

"I know," he admitted with a sigh. "Think you could wire
me some cash?"

Kaufman rented a sputtering moped that belched smoke and
sounded like a weed whacker. He peeled out of the crowded lot
into heavy, honking traffic.

Ragged Kaufman weaved his scooter through congested
city streets, choking on plumes of leaded exhaust. He eventually made his way to a bland, white office; one of twenty five
belonging to MONUSCO, the United Nations mission in the
DRC.

He cringed before locking the bike. The sun was setting,
and even in the nice part of town, it would still be nighttime in
the Congo.

Kaufman plodded into the office, hacking carbon particles
out of his lungs. His skin relaxed at the cool gust of air that greeted him. Kaufman had forgotten the sweet relief of climate control, but he resolved not to get too comfortable.

An overworked secretary looked up from her computer
and sighed.

"How may I help you?"

"I'm here to report a humanitarian crisis."

She blinked in disbelief for a few seconds, then nodded her
head. "Please take a seat." She assumed he was unwell. Surely no
mentally sound person would traipse in to make naive procla-
mations. It would be more newsworthy to report the absence of
crises. She hoped he'd eventually be distracted by the voices in his
head and wander out of her sight.

Kaufman shot her a dirty look. Didn't she realize it was an emergency?

Hours later, Kaufman was still drumming his fingers on a side table, grinding his teeth in mounting irritation.

"Listen, something needs to be done about the killing in Lualaba."

"I am just a receptionist. I cannot stop the killing in Lualaba, just as I cannot stop it in Kinshasa, or Uganda, or Somalia, or Rwanda, or Sudan or New York for that matter."

"So let me talk to someone who can!" Kaufman bellowed. Her eyes widened and she finally pushed the intercom button, lest the crazy man lash out at her.

Kaufman found himself sitting across from an impatient bureaucrat with a pencil-thin mustache and a grey polyester suit.

"This is not how it works, young sir." The paper pusher was amused. "We are not a police force. We do not take unilateral action." He checked his watch. "If you are hoping for peacekeeping intervention, perhaps you should call your congressman back home and ask him to have your U.N. Representative bring this matter up in the next Security Council meeting; then the member states can vote..." Kaufman huffed and stormed out. He should have known better, but desperation drove him to do absurd things.

He marched out of the U.N. Building and unsurprisingly the moped was gone. He sighed in resignation and trudged down the deserted sidewalk with his hands stuffed in his pockets. The once-lively avenue quickly emptied out upon nightfall. Only trouble stalked the streets at this hour.

A young punk spotted him from a dank alley and the proverbial cash registers rang in his eyes. The juvenile delinquent strutted out and blocked Kaufman's path.

"Give me your wallet." The boy made a mad-dog face at Kaufman, who rolled his eyes in mild irritation.

"Jump off a cliff." Had this been a month earlier, back in New York, Kaufman would have handed his billfold over in supplicating panic. But he had since stared down far scarier demons and wasn't about to surrender to a petty miscreant.

"I am not playing games," the punk warned. He pulled a rusty shank out of his pocket and waved it in Kaufman's face. Without thinking, Kaufman swiftly kicked the scumbag hard in the knee cap, making an audible crack. The punk collapsed, screeching like a wounded cat and Kaufman kept walking.

Writhing in pain, the boy threw his knife at Kaufman's back, but missed and the blade lamely scraped across the pavement. Kaufman didn't bother to turn around.

Kaufman shivered at a bus station at the side of a desolate street. His stupid plan had imploded and it was time to improvise. A rickety bus came to a squealing stop and Kaufman boarded.

An ancient driver closed the door and drove. His sunken eyes darted impatiently at the till.

"I want to buy the bus," Kaufman deadpanned.

The driver hit the brakes, throwing a pair of tired riders off balance. His bony hand pulled the lever to open the door.

"Get out." He had no patience for drug-addled foreigners.

Kaufman reached into his pocket and started plopping down hundred dollar bills, one by one, until he had amassed a few grand. The driver stared at the money in disbelief. For him, it was a decade's salary.

"Everybody off!" He screamed at the other passengers. At first they were frozen in disbelief. He gestured frantically, waving them out with trembling arms, lest Kaufman change his mind. They eventually realized he wasn't joking and grudgingly filed off, puzzled and annoyed, cursing him under their breath.

"I won't report it stolen for a week." The driver snatched the wad of cash and dashed out, gleefully running down the street as fast as his old bones could take him.

Kaufman closed the door and hit the gas, pulling a clumsy U-turn in the middle of the street. He found the switch that made the route sign say "Out of Service."

He stopped at a gas station at the very edge of town and bought several rusty jerry cans to fill with extra diesel. Kaufman stacked the combustible vessels in the last few rows of seats. It was a horible risk, but he had no choice – there would be scant opportunities to refuel in the middle of the green expanse.

27

Day and night, Kaufman rumbled toward Ulindi with no time to spare. He floored the decrepit bus across narrow, bumpy paths. It almost rolled over several times. He hoped the weight of the children would at least keep the rubber on the road.

The motor smoked and cried out with ungodly grinding noises. He would slow down just long enough to drop the engine temperature a few degrees before starting the abuse anew. He had to push it, since his friends were living on borrowed time. The vehicle reminded him of a cancerous old man, whose organs were failing in a cascading chain reaction.

The infernal motor would eventually blow a gasket, which would flood the pistons, which would contaminate the oil, which would further raise the temperature, which would melt the filter, which would splinter into the cooling system and clog it until the machine broiled itself from within and nothing would be left to salvage. It was a time bomb. Kaufman only hoped the old beast could complete this final mission.

Kaufman shuttled past rebel strongholds with such sloppy abandon that the guerrillas were befuddled at the sight of him. They didn't think to hold up the bus until it was long gone.

The coach emerged from the jungle and hobbled down dirt thoroughfares. Ulindi Village was a dusty ghost town and Kaufman feared the worst. Not only were the children absent, but no living soul stirred among the thatch-roofed huts. It was certainly possible that one of the villagers at the rally was Makanga's paid informant. Had the general already ordered their slaughter? That seemed improbable, since the homes were all intact. Had he halted his scorched-earth policy? That was even less likely. The man could never resist the sick thrill of destruction, nor would he bother disposing of his victim's bodies. Perhaps the entire village had escaped en masse?

The bus reached the desolate square and Kaufman felt a glimmer of hope. The youngest living child soldier kicked a can around in boredom. The little boy heard the jalopy sputter toward him and he petrified in mid-stride. He looked up at the vehicle, mesmerized like a deer caught in headlights. Kaufman stopped the bus and leapt out.

"Where is everyone?"

"Hiding, as you told us to," the child looked guilty – like he was caught disobeying orders. Apparently they took his request to lay low quite literally. The villagers were also spooked into playing along.

"Where's Sebu? We need to conceal this monster 'til nightfall."

The boy looked back up at the ungainly transport and blinked in disbelief.

They roused the children from their hiding places and tucked the bus in a ditch, clumsily camouflaging it with palm fronds.

They would wait until sundown and cross as many kilometers as they could under the cover of darkness. Without snags, the relative safety of the border was only a couple days' drive away. But they knew there would be snags.

At the first twinkle of starlight, Sebu and Kaufman brushed off the cover of leaves, as the children filed into the bus with their rifles slung on their shoulders.

"I fear we'll be caught," Sebu confessed.

"We can stay off major roads and cross the border far away from checkpoints — somewhere in the middle of nowhere." Kaufman shared Sebu's concern, but stifled it for morale.

"This pile of junk can't go far off the road." Sebu kicked a wheel and the whole suspension wobbled.

"What road? Look, we'll get as close as we can, then ditch it. We'll cross on foot."

Sebu looked Kaufman in the eye and cracked a sad smile. "Wouldn't you rather be back in New York, drinking hot chocolate and playing with your computers?"

"Of course. Wouldn't you?"

Sebu laughed wistfully. They boarded the bus and drove into the night.

Kaufman pushed the pedal to the floor and still the behemoth struggled under the weight of all the added bodies. At least it wouldn't roll. The bus trembled and shook, its shock absorbers battered against the pockmarked road.

"If Makanga doesn't kill us, this bus will," Lumumba groaned.

Soon all the children were car sick. They clutched their weapons, as if bullets could ward off nausea. The air was thick with tension. No one made a sound.

Kaufman's eyes were glued to the road as he struggled to stay on course. If his focus wavered for a second, he could easily drive them into a river or off a cliff. But he looked back for a moment and saw the children trembling like caged rabbits. He had to blow off some steam:

"The wheels on the bus go round and round; round and round; round and round. The wheels on the bus go round and round; all the live-long day..." The children stared at Kaufman like he was smoking brown-brown. What was this bizarre ditty he belted off key?

Hours later, Kaufman somehow had all the children singing: "The wipers on the bus go swish, swish, swish; Swish, swish, swish; Swish, swish, swish. The wipers on the bus go swish, swish, swish, all through the town..." They still clutched their weapons like security blankets.

The sun rose as the children sang a Congolese song. They had made it through the night without incident and were gradually allowing themselves to feel a hint of optimism.

The beater sped past a depressed village, perpetually at the brink of starvation from constant pillaging by one faction or another. The elder spotted the bus full of singing, armed children and his eyes bugged. For his collaboration, he stood to reap a handsome reward and protection for his community – or so he thought. His real future was far less rosy. The chief rushed to a shack and pried the communal cell phone from a gossiping woman.

A few miles down the road, the children were finally starting to tire and doze. Kaufman let out a sigh of relief. Then he gasped.

"Sebu!" He elbowed the poor boy in the ribs just as he crossed the threshold into dreamland.

Sebu jolted alert and spotted a hastily erected roadblock in the distance, manned by a couple of Makanga's soldiers. He nudged Lumumba, who panicked at the sight of them.

Lumumba leapt up and heaved down a window, about to aim his AK-47 out the side. "There are only two men. We can shoot them from here."

"It is too risky," Sebu warned. "This bus is a death trap. We must fan out." If one stray bullet hit a jerry can in the back, they'd all be broiled inside a rolling fireball.

"Let's not get ahead of ourselves." Kaufman scrambled to think of a better way. He called back to the children: "Hide your weapons and play along.

The children erupted in dissent.

"Trust me," he implored. "Have I ever let you down?"

They grudgingly slid their rifles under their seats. Kaufman prayed he wouldn't fail them now.

His hands trembled as he pulled up to the checkpoint, smiling like a jackass, at the guards.

"I'm with the Peace Corps Orphanage. We're going on a field trip." He gave his best impression of a well-meaning, corn-fed Mormon.

"I must inspect," the soldier was incredulous.

"By all means." Kaufman's voice cracked under feigned ease.

One merc stayed back, suspiciously eying Kaufman, while his colleague boarded the bus. Their safeties were off and their itchy fingers rested on their triggers. Kaufman and the children all tried to muffle their thumping hearts.

The mercenary crept cautiously up the stairs and scanned the children, who all appeared to be well behaved, with their hands neatly folded in their laps.

"They are all orphans?"

"Yeah, want to adopt some? I'll give you two for the price of one."

The fighter manhandled one of the children, as if checking a horse for head-lice and tooth decay. "Yes please, I have so much love to give," he deadpanned.

He spotted the corner of a rifle stock sticking out from under a seat and panicked. The spooked merc planted his foot on the weapon, then swung his gun around at Kaufman. He suddenly felt ten barrels jammed against his head. The boys cycled their AK-47s for emphasis.

The second mercenary outside lifted his rifle, but froze when he saw several more children with Kalashnikovs already trained on his head.

"Everybody relax." Kaufman held his sweaty palms up in a gesture of appeasement. For some reason he was still nervous. He was certain they had the upper hand, that they could easily execute these horrible men and be on their merry way. But he also knew that if the children kept sinking down the rabbit hole of hate and violence, they'd never be able to claw themselves back out. "We're going to deal with this situation like rational human beings and all of us will live to see another day." The mercs couldn't believe their ears – they expected to already be dead.

The boys stuffed the guards in a fetid outhouse and fastened their wrists and ankles with duct tape. Kaufman put a strip on each of their mouths, both so they couldn't scream and also so they would be punished to breathe through their noses.

"See how civil we all can be? Now I'm relying on your good-will and maybe your sense of pride, not to tell anyone that you got hog-tied by a bunch of schoolchildren."

"I wish we could go to school," Lumumba lamented.

"School-aged children," Kaufman somberly corrected himself.

The bound warmongers nodded vigorously, happy to be alive. Kaufman and the boys locked them in the stinking latrine, jumped into their rolling ark and sped away.

The children cheered their bloodless coup. Kaufman floored his engine again and let the bus bounce and wobble over rough road. For all he knew, Makanga's reinforcements might already have been en route, so he had ever more reason to hastily disappear.

He excitedly whipped his attention back and forth from the road to the kids in the back.

"That was pretty good, right?"

They nodded.

"See – if you keep reaching for your rifle to solve your problems, you won't have long to live. Eventually, you will be outgunned. But your most dangerous weapon – your most useful tool – is your mind."

The children were starting to see things his way.

Then the bus ground to a halt.

28

They trudged out to find the hood belching smoke.

"Why can't anything go right for more than ten minutes?" Kaufman asked no one.

"You were too pleased with yourself," Lumumba explained. He let out a fatalistic sigh. "Whenever I think I'm good at anything, life shows me otherwise."

Kaufman nodded – since touching down on the continent, that had certainly been the case. He reached out to pop the hood and scorched his hand. He screamed and yanked it back. His red, throbbing skin would soon bubble and blister.

Lumumba lifted a stick and used it to pry the hood. A gust of smoke rushed out and engulfed them. They coughed and violently heaved, their faces filling with tears and mucus. The radiator puked steaming green fluid into the dirt.

"No more whining," Sebu ordered. "Now we march."

Kaufman and the children fanned out on a calm plain, trekking through tall grass that swayed in a gentle wind. The air was clean. They passed blue, cloud-capped mountains and herds of zebra grazing in the distance. Birds were singing and there wasn't another godforsaken human being in sight.

"What will you do once you are free?" A boy asked Sebu.

"I don't know. Kaufman, what exactly do you do?"

"I'm a securities analyst."

"What's that?"

"I sit in an office all day staring at computer screens, trying to outsmart people sitting in similar offices all over the world. They make huge bets on everything from the future price of soybeans to interest rate differentials... I basically make rich people richer."

"Definitely not that!" The children laughed. Kaufman was starting to share the sentiment.

"Maybe I can be a teacher," Lumumba mused.

"You already are," Kaufman sighed. Lumumba didn't understand.

"I think we're almost at the border," Sebu gathered. A wave of excited chatter shot through the ranks. For a shining moment, all their hearts were weightless.

Then Lumumba felt a metallic click under his foot. He looked down to see an orange bloom erupt from the ground and engulf his leg in fire. The landmine blasted his lanky frame into the air. He flailed earthward and landed on his back with a crunch.

Panicked children rushed to his aid, crying and screaming their little heads off.

"Freeze!" Kaufman shouted. They halted where they stood. "This place is a disaster."

"You just noticed?" Lumumba groaned. The pain hadn't fully hit him. He was in shock and couldn't really feel anything.

Sebu held his breath. He wasn't there. He was outside himself, watching the horrific scene from above. He didn't allow himself to entertain the possibility of Lumumba dying. He had already lost his best friend once.

Kaufman grabbed a rifle from the nearest boy, averted his face and poked at the earth between Lumumba and himself. He stepped gingerly over and crouched at Lumumba's side.

Lumumba's leg was shredded like hamburger meat, hemorrhaging blood. Kaufman knew it couldn't be salvaged, but he prayed the rest of him could. He tore his sleeve and fashioned a tourniquet.

Lumumba screamed as Kaufman tightened the fabric around his thigh. Feeling rushed back to his leg like a freight train and the agony was all-consuming. Every nerve in his body was on fire – there was even phantom pain from the nerves he no longer had.

Kaufman looked over his shoulder to see Sebu and the children looking ashen. Their faces were wide eyed in shock and denial.

"Stop bleeding," Kaufman begged of Lumumba's wounds. But they kept gushing, coating the earth in deep crimson. Lumumba started to shiver. He no longer had enough blood to keep his body warm.

Sebu came back into himself and everyone gasped as he recklessly ran over and crouched at Lumumba's other side. Kaufman and Lumumba pressed their hands on the wounds, but they just got drenched in blood. Sebu stifled tears.

"Please hang on!" Sebu begged his friend. Lumumba wished he could, but he felt himself slipping away. His vision grew blurry, his eyes were glassy and distant.

"I'm scared," Lumumba whispered.

"Me too," Sebu confessed.

Kaufman scrambled frantically to tighten the tourniquet, but deep down he knew it was futile.

Lumumba felt cold and weightless. His breath came in short gasps, his vision narrowed to a single point of light. And then he was gone.

Sebu's tears burst forth like a dam was broken inside him. His body convulsed with grief. Kaufman hung his head.

Kaufman struggled to dig a grave with his bare hands. The soil was packed hard and he didn't make much progress. Dirt lodged in his oozing blisters. A boy joined him, then another. They were scratching lamely at the earth, stubbing their fingers on rocks. The sun would soon set and they would have even more trouble avoiding mines.

Sebu figured Makanga's men must have discovered the abandoned bus by now. They were probably being tracked. He could not afford to mourn – he was accountable for the living. They had to vanish.

"Stop it," he ordered with a heavy heart.

Kaufman looked up at Sebu and saw his quivering face struggling to hold back more tears.

"We must do this or we'll regret it forever." Kaufman returned to frantically scratch at his shallow pit.

"There is no time. We go now, or we won't live to regret anything." Sebu turned and walked away without looking back. He knew what Lumumba would have wanted. The boys somberly followed their commander. Kaufman reluctantly left the boy lying next to a tree.

Sebu hoped the animals wouldn't find him. He hoped that Lumumba would be absorbed into the earth, that his body would nourish the plants, that their pollen would spread a little part of him across the land and his spirit would be everywhere – inhaled and exhaled by every living thing. Perhaps one day there would be peace and Lumumba would surround them all.

Kaufman and the children raced the setting sun, trudging in a straight line in somber silence. Kaufman took the lead, jabbing the earth ahead of them with a long stick, not really sure if this improvisation would protect them from a blast.

He did eventually hit another mine, which flung the wood out of his hands and almost stabbed him in the head. The children gasped. Kaufman groaned. He took a little shrapnel in the shin, but was far enough away to miss the brunt of it. He picked the shards of jagged metal from runny gashes in his flesh, but there was no time to really clean the wounds.

"Someone hand me another stick," he called back.

They passed a branch forward and resumed the march.

"This is my duty." Sebu tried to take over Kaufman's perilous task. Perhaps a part of him wanted to join his friend.

"I have longer arms." Kaufman forged ahead.

The boys heard something vaguely unnatural far behind them. Was it a vehicle? As the vibrations grew closer, they knew there were several. Everyone panicked. Kaufman heard the whirr of chopper blades in the distance. Then the rumble of diesel engines approached. They desperately scanned their surroundings and saw nothing. But they heard trees crashing earthward and animals screeching and scrambling in terror.

"Run! We can't be far from the border." Sebu charged past Kaufman. They could no longer afford the luxury of caution. They dashed through the tall grass as unseen war machines roared louder and closer.

Another boy hit a mine and launched skyward in a fountain of fire. The children broke ranks and scattered in pandemonium as the blitzkrieg bore down on them.

"Hide!" Kaufman gasped.

They dove into the tall grass and cowered. The thundering growl of combustion kept rushing toward them. Kaufman prayed that they would remain unseen as the monsters rolled past. But they were not so lucky. Mechanized hell broke loose.

A single helicopter lifted above the horizon and hovered directly over them. It blew the grass aside in waves and exposed the tops of their cowering heads. Kaufman looked up and was surprised to see it wasn't a military aircraft. It was more like the luxurious, black executive choppers his colleagues chartered for jaunts to Martha's Vineyard.

Armored Humvees bounded up over the hill and encircled Kaufman and the boys. Mercenaries gleefully spilled out of the transports and pointed their weapons into the grass where the children hid. The boys didn't dare pull their weapons, since they were all pinned, with beads drawn on their heads.

The commander swaggered out of the lead vehicle, relieved to finally have them in his grasp. They had been so slippery and had caused him so much stress – he couldn't wait to snap their little necks. He was so confident in his victory, he did not carry a rifle, nor did he brandish his sidearm.

"Mr. Kaufman, please come out and have a little chat with us." He patronized him with mock politeness.

Trembling, Kaufman stood to face the music, his arms aloft in surrender. He wondered if they would shoot him where he stood, or torture him first. The commander nodded at the chopper and it touched down next to them. Two burly, white agents in dark suits and sunglasses stepped out of the aircraft and strode over. Kaufman knew who pulled the strings to get them there.

"Mr. Kaufman, we've been asked to return you to the States," one agent flatly informed him.

"I can't leave them."

"You have no choice."

"Please take the children too!" Kaufman pleaded.

"We have our orders."

The other agent snaked behind and cuffed him. Kaufman tried to slip free, but of course it was no use. They were trained to snatch far more formidable prey.

"You know what'll happen to those kids? Can you live with it?" Kaufman screamed in desperation. The mercs had a good chuckle.

"Son, you're in too deep," the agent whispered through gritted teeth.

"Spook, I'm not your son. Get your hands off me."

They dragged him kicking and screaming into the helicopter. He looked back in terror as the mercenaries manhandled the children out of their hiding places in the grass and shoved them into a flatbed truck.

The helicopter was airborne again, whisking Kaufman away as quickly as it came. The pilot never even cut the rotors.

The interior of the craft was insulated from sound and wrapped in supple leather. Writhing in his restraints, Kaufman glared at the agents.

"Who sent you?" Kaufman already knew the answer – he just wanted to hear it.

"We're not at liberty to say."

"You know they'll be killed?!" Kaufman looked out the window and saw the dreaded soldiers roughing up the kids. Sebu glanced up and made eye contact with Kaufman. His face looked helpless and wistful.

"It's not our place to speculate," the agent answered dispassionately.

"I'm not speculating. It's pretty obvious."

"We can't help them."

"Then what the hell are you good for?"

"For taking you home."

29

The boys huddled together like frightened rabbits, trembling at gunpoint in the bouncing truck bed. The vehicle raced back to headquarters at top speed, taking to the air every time it hit a bump. The mercenaries' twitchy fingers rested on their triggers. It was a bloodbath waiting to happen.

The children watched hopelessly as the helicopter receded until it was mere a spec on the horizon – and then it was gone forever. They had seen Kaufman's worried face pressed against the glass, but now they could see nothing. What a strange man he was, from another world, who followed them on their final, ill-fated mission.

The boys tried to savor the last impressions of their beloved homeland – they felt the rainforest mist against their faces; the tickle and fragrance of pollen in their nostrils; the view of rich verdure as far as their eyes could see; the calls of animals and the buzz of insects. They knew these familiar sensations would soon be wrenched away.

Bang – a rifle accidentally discharged and scared the boys out of their skins. They checked their bodies for leaking holes, but found themselves intact.

"Sorry – bad road," A gap-toothed merc snickered.

His comrades broke out laughing.

"Careful! They are worth more alive. Makanga wants them all to suffer before they die," the commander chided.

The children shuddered, but Sebu did not flinch. He was immersed in thought, contemplating what Kaufman had told them a few hours before:

"If you keep reaching for your rifle to solve your problems, you won't have long to live. Eventually, you will be outgunned. But your most dangerous weapon; your most useful tool is your mind."

But what clever parlor trick could possibly get them out of this bind? They were watched like hawks and all it took was a bent index finger to wipe them out.

The mercenaries paraded the terrified boys, their small wrists bound tight, into Makanga's stately mansion. They prodded the children along with pomp and swagger. The servants were puzzled by the spectacle – all they saw was a ragged band of urchins. They looked pityingly at the corralled captives – they knew what grisly fate awaited them, and unlike the battle-hardened killers, they still felt a twinge of pity in their hearts. These were the children of their ancestral villages.

Despite their mortal terror, the boys could not help but marvel at the opulence packed into each encrusted square inch of the estate. Every handle and molding was intricately designed and mirror-polished so not even a stray fingerprint could be found. They gaped at paintings and sculptures that were so lifelike; they were a window to another reality. The little ragamuffins had never imagined such treasures could even exist. If their hours weren't numbered, they'd have something to aspire to. The general had so much – what did he want with them?

They were tossed like garbage at Makanga's feet and shoved down to their knees. He towered over them on a gilded throne, flanked by red-eyed guards. Makanga deigned to step down from his self-made altar, caressing the ornate Colt .45 at his belt. He immediately recognized the boy who almost ended him.

"My Prodigal Son — you have returned to me." His ogrish hand savagely grabbed Sebu by the chin and pulled him upright, to glare into his eyes.

Sebu scowled back, stone faced. He was scared out of his mind, but he would not give Makanga the satisfaction of knowing.

"Perhaps if you beg forgiveness, I'll make your deaths less painful," Makanga taunted.

A couple of the younger boys groveled and scraped. Sebu scowled and they clammed up, out of respect for their leader.

"Perhaps I'll give you a reason to let us all go free." Sebu conjured uncanny conviction to sell his pitch. Their only chance was a bold confidence game. Sebu couldn't betray a hint of doubt, or the plan would fall apart.

Makanga unleashed a deep belly laugh. He beckoned a sweaty, muscle-bound dog-of-war, who unsheathed a rusty machete. "You have nothing of value to me," Makanga snorted. His henchman held the dull blade aloft to hack Sebu's head off.

All the children winced. The air escaped from their lungs. They could not bear to see their leader cut down before them. Without Sebu, there would be no hope.

He somehow held his ground. "A man as smart as you knows the value of information," Sebu cajoled. There was something uncanny and enticing in his voice. Makanga couldn't bring himself to slay the child quite yet.

"What do you know?" Makanga raised an eyebrow.

"How can I be sure you won't kill us?"

"You can't. But if you don't give me anything, I certainly will. And it will be painful."

"I found new mineral deposits in the jungle — far richer than your measly coltan. But you must make us partners in the mine."

Makanga grinned at Sebu's insolence. He would enjoy disemboweling the boy and strangling him with his own intestines.

The children were crammed into a dank cellar and locked away to spend their final night like animals in a slaughterhouse, breathing stagnant, musty air and sharing a single, rancid waste bucket. They were given a jerry can of scummy water and a few moldy, raw potatoes.

Their little hearts would be left to beat just long enough for Sebu to divulge his secrets and then they would be butchered in the most demented ways, to entertain the mercs who spilled sweat and blood to catch them. Makanga planned a sadistic circus that would have even made the Romans wretch.

The children groped every inch of their dungeon, in the dark, searching for a weakness or potential escape route, but there was none. They were desperate and angry. Boys started turning on each other, bickering over elbow room and rotten rations.

"Stop that," Sebu ordered. "It's exactly what they want us to do. Remember who you are."

"What minerals, Sebu?" A little boy seemed hurt that he had held out on them.

"You know – the rich platinum deposits. Maybe if the mine is bountiful, the President will let us live." Sebu spoke very loudly, while glaring at the boy and pointing up at the cellar door. "I'm sure they're listening," he whispered in the boy's ear.

He gathered them into a close huddle. "I want you all to know how honored I am to have fought and bled alongside you," he whispered just loudly enough that only they could hear. "Whatever happens tomorrow, we should be proud – that we didn't believe the rebels' lies, that we were brave, that we did what we knew was right. We may come from different villages and different families, but we are all brothers. I love you like I love myself."

Their hearts beat as one.

30

It was a sunny, spring day in Manhattan. People had cast off their cocoons of layered wool and showed off their skin and elevated spirits, after a long, dark winter. But Kaufman was numb. Milos had urged him to take some days off, but the last thing he needed was time and space to clear his mind and reflect. It took every possible distraction to keep the flood of regret from drowning him.

Kaufman was still contractually bound to secrecy. The Jupiter Fund could not be linked to other people's war crimes. They had a fiduciary duty to their investors to uphold the tenuous pretext of ignorance; or at least plausible deniability. So Kaufman couldn't even indulge in the catharsis of confession.

He set foot on the frenzied trading floor and everyone abruptly halted what they were doing, to break into a thunderous standing ovation. Kaufman felt his stomach sink. Were they mocking him? Did they somehow know he failed to save his friends? Or were the bastards actually proud of how he had conducted himself in the perilous jungle?

In truth, the traders had no idea where he had gone or what he had done. They were just happy to have their meal ticket back. Returns had slumped considerably in his absence. Mistakes were made that he could have prevented. His presence had a direct effect on all their lifestyles – their children's tony private school tuition, their wives' spa memberships, their conspicuous consumption of scotch and hookers.

"Thank God you're back, buddy." Chaz was first to clap his shoulder. He was nearly fired in Kaufman's absence, but now he expected job security and smooth sailing for the foreseeable future.

"Where did do you go, Bro? Rehab?" Derrick elbowed him in the ribs. "We'll all make sure to keep you off the dust, if it keeps you in the office." A couple traders cracked up, hugging Kaufman like they were old friends.

Catatonic Kaufman couldn't take it. He turned and retreated to his cloistered office. A hush descended on the killing floor. The traders prayed they hadn't driven him away for good.

Milos had been watching it all from his lofted vantage point, scrutinizing Kaufman's mood, his reactions, his subtle tics and gestures. Everything was riding on Kaufman's compliance. Milos pondered what kind of incentives; or disincentives, if necessary, he could offer to ensure his cooperation.

Kaufman slouched in front of his screens, staring blankly at securities dancing up and down the charts. The monitors cast a dull glow against his sickly face. His eyes were dark, puffy and bloodshot; his skin was dry and brittle. He hadn't eaten or slept in days.

He checked on the old mainstays – the euro, gold, oil, treasury bills, S&P futures, etc. They were all more or less where he left them. In the sanitized retrospect of the charts, he saw that prices had churned and swung violently in his absence, but ultimately went nowhere. He knew that millions of people had worked themselves into a frenzy, following every tick on their screens, cultivating hypertension and stomach ulcers, poisoning their bodies and minds with stress. They obsessed over gyrations of fractions of a penny, amplified by billions of shares. Vast fortunes were won and lost every second. The upswings were a drunken orgy of celebration, while the drops were punctuated with melodrama and teeth gnashing. Some people continued trading in their dreams. The markets were so fraught with sound and fury, but ultimately signified nothing.

Traders treated their jobs like they were a matter of life or death. But if they had seen what Kaufman had, the price of pork bellies wouldn't mean much to them anymore. Life and death would take on a far more intimate meaning.

Milos peeked into Kaufman's office with uncharacteristic humility and gentleness. The man was not made of stone. He knew what Kaufman had endured and he knew it was all his fault. Sterling took the seat across from Kaufman and peered deep into his pained eyes.

"You can understand why I had to pull you out of there?"

A small fraction of Kaufman returned to the room. His eyes focused briefly on Milos' rugged, weathered face. He wondered how many geopolitical incidents Sterling had a hand in. He wondered how far the nationless king could reach.

Kaufman betrayed the slightest hint of a nod. Milos forced a sympathetic smile, stood and exited.

"Mr. Sterling," Kaufman called out after him.

Milos returned.

"Why on earth would you get in bed with an African Warlord?"

Milos was taken aback. No one had addressed him so forwardly in years. But it was a fair question.

An eternity passed in a moment, as Sterling reflected on his mistakes. Kaufman's anger simmered.

Finally, Milos opened his mouth and let out the faintest whisper: "I'm just a man." He shrugged contritely, stood and left Kaufman to churn through his feelings.

31

The monstrous convoy rumbled through delicate jungle paths, crushing every living thing in its way. Armored Humvees punched a hole for Makanga's limousine to coast through. The regular swarm of motorcycling mercenaries surrounded a filthy fruit truck, overloaded with orphans held at gunpoint.

They unknowingly roared by a macabre Mai-Mai totem.

Sebu sat across from Makanga in the Limousine, squeezed between hulking guards. The general needed Sebu there to give directions as they penetrated deeper into the uncharted backwoods of his homeland.

But what he really wanted was to see the boy squirm, to laugh as he begged for mercy, to make him blubber and cry, to watch him tremble and sweat and lose control of his faculties. He wanted to dominate him, to break his spirit, to extract every last ounce of strength from his limbs. He wanted to crush each cell in Sebu's body, to dissolve his flesh into its essential chemicals, to wipe the final trace of the insolent child from the earth.

No one had ever thwarted Makanga so perfectly. Sebu mucked up the deal that would have established his dominion over the entire region. No one had ever succeeded in shooting the general. Not only had the boy scarred Makanga's body with a bullet, but he also insinuated himself deep under his skin. He made Makanga feel something he hadn't felt for years – fear.

Fear made him weak and vulnerable. It reminded him that he was not some omnipotent God, but a mere mortal like everyone else; who was lucky enough to grab some power for the time being, who could be destroyed just as easily as he could destroy others. For that humbling reminder, Makanga's hate for Sebu was infinite – it flowed in colossal volume and undying force – like the Congo River itself. It poisoned Makanga and everything around him.

Of course Sebu was terrified, but he counted himself dead already. He focused on his breathing. He paralyzed his facial muscles to deprive Makanga of a window to his feelings. He could sense the monster's hate searing him like fires of hell. Makanga's face was intimately close. He smelled the beast's acrid breath – it reeked as if he had been feasting on corpses. But Sebu would not give the criminal the satisfaction of seeing him flinch.

His final gambit relied on self-assurance. He had to project the foolish notion that he believed what he had to offer Makanga was so valuable, that in exchange, he and his brothers would be spared. Why else would he give up the priceless secret?

"If the mine is rich, I may let you boys live," Makanga taunted. "To harvest my treasure until you collapse."

Sebu play-acted sighing in relief. "Turn left at the fork," he exclaimed.

No one saw a fearsome, painted Mai-Mai warrior leap out of the bushes and sprint alongside the limo in a low crouch. The wild-eyed man tracked their trajectory for a brief moment before diving back into the brush.

The convoy battered through the tree line and trespassed on a secluded clearing, untouched by machines since the beginning of time. Sebu directed them to cut their belching engines at the top of an ancient crater, now overgrown with foliage. He was shoved out at gunpoint and led Makanga to peer over the ledge.

"It's all down there. More wealth than you ever dreamed of!" Sebu screamed, feigning irrepressible excitement. He darted desperate glances at the surrounding jungle.

Makanga squinted incredulously at the depths of the pit. He pointed his pistol at Sebu's skull and pulled back the hammer. "You have delayed enough."

Sebu couldn't stall much longer – something had to happen fast. "Let me show you," the boy pleaded. His charade of cool-headedness had run its course. He called out at the top of his lungs, in hopes that someone may hear his offense. "You will have to cut down this jungle and kill all the locals, but there is great treasure to be ripped from the earth." Sebu snuck another peek at the rainforest, but saw no one. He did hear the distressed squawking of birds. He prayed they weren't just scared of the soldiers; that something more sinister was coming for them.

Makanga rolled his eyes and gestured for his shock troops to escort them down. He had the luxury of killing Sebu whenever he wanted – he might as well hear what the little rat had to say.

Only two scrawny guards stayed behind to detain the boys on the truck. After all, it would only take one to mow them down in a torrent of gunfire.

In the depths of the basin, Makanga stomped on the hardened ground. "This rocky earth has nothing." He pressed his weapon against Sebu's forehead. "How can I punish you extra for wasting my time? Shall I feed you your own liver?"

The last shred of Sebu's composure had fizzled. "No! Just tear down the forest, purge the local savages and you will find more platinum than you could ever dream of. The American told me how to mine it. Your coltan pits won't even be worth digging. You can build a modern city on this land and people will trample through the jungle to work for you." Sebu screamed as loudly as his little lungs would push. He gesticulated frantically. He looked up at the

edge of the cliff, but it was still silent and empty. The boy was
trapped in a great pit of dirt – what a horrible place to die.

Makanga smiled, finally satisfied to see the boy crack. "Perhaps the child was useful after all," he snickered at his goons.

Sebu made no more pretext of speaking to Makanga, but
roared his threat up into the jungle. Someone had to heed his
cries. "Yes, I will be very useful. I will help you kill the Mai-Mai."

"No, you have done enough for me," Makanga chuckled.
"You are no longer needed. You have worked so hard – it is time
for you to rest." Makanga shoved his golden pistol between Sebu's
eyes. His finger hesitated – he felt the bloodlust boiling up, to kill
Sebu where he stood, but he also wanted to see him suffer more.

His quiet indecision was broken by a shrill battle cry rever-
berating through the basin. The birds took flight, frantically flap-
ping to escape the cursed place. Even the inveterate war criminals
were now gripped with mortal terror. Inhuman screams rattled
their eardrums and shook them to the core. Makanga looked up
but saw nothing at first.

Outside the basin, heavy, sharpened pikes hurled through
the air and rammed through the gangly guards' hearts, erupting
them into fountains of blood and tissue. Their bodies crumpled
like flimsy rag dolls. The terrified children crouched flat against
the soiled truck bed, trembling.

Mai-Mai warriors swarmed out of the jungle in droves, like
a hive of angry bees and sprinted at the pit. Their voices melded
into a single, high-pitched, skin-crawling drone.

Inside the chasm, Makanga was overcome with dread. The
wily little snake had led him into a trap. This could be the end.
At the very least he would drag Sebu with him down to hell.
He squeezed the trigger but Sebu dove out of the way. The stray
shot struck one of his soldiers in the leg. The mercenary yelped
and bled, but Makanga was not concerned with him. The general
re-fixed his aim on Sebu, when a volley of stones rained down

on them, cracking open mercenary heads, their bodies collapsing and piling up on the floor of the basin. Makanga and Sebu barely survived the first wave.

They looked up and saw the cliff lined with painted Mai-Mai militia in gaudy battle regalia, towering over them. Their faces were snarled in territorial aggression. The Mai-Mai looked down and glared at Makanga and his mercs. The soldiers looked so small, pinned to the bottom of the basin.

Makanga aimed his pistol up and squeezed off a few rounds. The mercenaries swung their rifles skyward and opened fire. Even a handful of men could unleash a deadly tidal-wave of metal with their Kalashnikovs on full-auto.

But the Mai-Mai simply stepped back out of sight as Makanga's men wasted bullets in the air. Some rounds dropped earthward and plunged through soldiers' skulls, with the same ease as pebbles splashing into water. Their lives and memories were effortlessly erased.

Sebu took the distraction as an opportunity to roll away and slither his slim frame into a crevice in the wall of the pit.

Makanga and his men were entirely exposed, like fish in a barrel, while the Mai-Mai had plenty of cover and higher ground. The unseen braves let out another blood curdling cry, as the mercenaries scrambled to reload.

Before the mercenaries could cock their rifles, an even deadlier volley rained down on them – this time with spears as well as rocks and an occasional shotgun blast for good measure. The mercenaries took more casualties before they could open fire again. They finally managed to kill a few Mai-Mai, who fell face first into the pit. Some of the warrior's corpses landed on the mercenaries and broke their necks.

The battle raged back and forth – the mercenaries with superior firepower and the Mai-Mai with a tactical advantage and far greater numbers.

Sebu watched the clash, still cowering in his hole. He did not care whether or not he'd survive — as long as he could watch Makanga die first. He thought of his family and the peaceful life he used to have. He thought of his fallen brothers and of Lumumba bleeding to death in the field. He prayed that he would exist just long enough to witness his nemesis defeated, to see his blood gush into the dirt, to look into the demon's eyes as he took his last, painful gasp and left the world forever.

Makanga spotted him hiding in the crag and the same all-consuming hate smoldered right back at Sebu. All his earthly ambitions narrowed to a pinpoint — he wanted Sebu dead.

"You clever little boy!" Makanga snarled. He aimed his .45 sidearm at Sebu's head and pulled the trigger.

Click — the magazine was empty. Makanga reached into his pocket to reload, and aimed at Sebu again. The boy shivered, closed his eyes and took a deep breath. His final, stunted wish would not come true. He would have cried, but he ran out of tears long ago.

Slash — Makanga was felled by a massive spear. His gun fired lamely at the wall of the pit, missing the boy by entirely.

Sebu did not have time to feel relief. The devil was not quite dead. Bleeding on the ground, his shaky hand struggled to raise the weapon again. He roared in fatal rage. Before he could fire, a huge stone landed on his head. His scream was snuffed by a sickly crunch. The last volley of spears extinguished the rest of his men.

At the top of the cliff, the frightened children raised their hands in surrender, but the Mai-Mai had no interest in them. They recovered their dead and evaporated into the foliage from whence they came.

Back in the basin, Sebu hesitantly emerged from his hole. He looked up with relief to see no more Mai-Mai looming overhead.

He kicked Makanga's lifeless body to make absolutely sure he would not rise again.

Sebu felt the weight of the universe lifted from his shoulders. It cost him everything, but his debt was finally paid. From that moment on, he was free.

A small boy peeked over the cliff. "Sebu?" The child cracked the hugest smile when he saw his leader still alive.

Sebu allowed himself a world-weary grin.

32

Kaufman hadn't marshaled the will to roll out of bed for several days now. Distraction had failed him and he plunged into a bottomless vortex of depression. The darkness was all-consuming – a black hole whose gravity he could not escape. He felt trapped forever, crushed from every angle. He wished he was dead.

Food tasted like nothing. Music sounded like noise. He reveled in stubbing his toe on the way to the toilet – the sting cut through the fog and felt like something.

Calls from the office went unanswered. He couldn't bring himself to speak to his parents, because he couldn't imagine how he would even begin to explain his misadventure.

He felt ashamed for being alive, when he was certain his young friends were dead. He felt guilty that he wasn't clever enough, quick enough or powerful enough to save them. He knew the same fate befell children in similar conflicts all over the developing world. That knowledge was now concrete and tangible to him.

He ignored a knock on the door; which gradually escalated to relentless thumping.

"Open up, Kaufman!" A gallingly familiar voice demanded.

"Let us in, you sneaky fox," a frisky female chirped. He also knew her from somewhere. Several more grating voices joined in, insisting that they be granted entry to his pit of despair.

He tried to wait it out, but eventually resigned himself to the fact that they weren't going anywhere. Kaufman strained his body upright and trudged to the door.

The traders and their model dates were horrified to witness his disheveled state.

"Holy crap, we need to fix this." Derrick gestured to Kaufman, head to toe. They spilled into his home.

"Milos said he won't let us into the Vulture's Feast without you." They shoved him toward the shower. "We dug up your special friend."

"Hi!" Carrie, Kaufman's last one-night-stand, fluttered her crimson tipped fingers and coquettishly batted her lashes. Her skimpy, silk dress barely covered her lithe frame. How did they find her? He wondered who had actually been paying attention when he took her home, what seemed like a lifetime ago.

Kaufman squirmed in his monkey suit in the back of a tacky Hummer limo. Sloppy drunk traders were already marauding their willing female victims. Carrie squeezed Kaufman's thigh.

"You never called."

"I was out of the country."

"Why didn't you take me?" She half joked – though she really would have agreed to tag along.

Kaufman couldn't help but laugh. If only she knew how that would have gone.

Kaufman trudged along with the exodus of plastered sycophants stumbling up Milos' sprawling lawn. Accompanied by a full brass band, they followed a path of glowing paper lanterns. The trail wound by barely dressed acrobats and fire breathers on stilts. Carrie hung on Kaufman's arm like an albatross. She was already walking barefoot, holding her strappy stilettos after they had repeatedly lodged in the turf.

Kaufman reached the vineyard and beheld clients and financiers shamelessly gorging themselves on lobster, caviar, filet mignon, pâté and truffles. They guzzled magnums of Cristal champagne and casks of ancient whisky. These people could afford to eat whatever they wanted, but they still wouldn't pass up a chance to pack their maws with freebies.

An orchestra dashed off string arrangements of pop songs, so old men could dance with their barely-legal paramours.

A sculptor carved a colossal Milos Sterling out of ice, in the heroic Soviet style – his body poised in a self-righteous march, his jaw enhanced and his eyes peering off into the distance.

Kaufman was nauseous – if there was anything in his stomach, he'd have trouble keeping it down.

"I never could have dreamed of a swank party like this back in Montana." Carrie was slack-jawed in amazement. Kaufman turned to her.

"Look, you seem like a nice girl. Can I give you some friendly advice? Go back to Montana and live like a normal human being before you lose the last shred of yourself. None of this is real."

"Yeah, I guess you're right," she paid him brief lip service, since he was her admission ticket. But she wasn't buying it. She clung a little tighter to his arm, intimidated by all the rainmakers and power brokers in her midst.

Kaufman pondered – if someone dropped a bunker buster and reduced the whole scene to a pile of smoldering rubble, would the world be a better place?

A temporary stage had been erected and a popular late-night host was helicoptered in from Manhattan to deliver a pre-approved standup comedy routine for exactly thirty minutes; before being whisked back and handed a cashier's check for half a million dollars. An aging adult-contemporary singer was shuttled in from Atlantic City for roughly the same deal.

Then Milos took the microphone and proceeded to pat himself and to a lesser extent, his underlings on the back – in a rambling speech, cheering their unrivaled trading returns and milking their proportionally sparse charitable contributions for all the goodwill they were worth. Kaufman suppressed a wave of nausea.

"Now I'm going to let you all in on our secret weapon," Milos whispered conspiratorially into the microphone and looked straight at Kaufman. "In recent years, we have all been deeply enriched by the genius of one young man – I don't just mean from his intellect and contributions to our bottom line – though both are considerable. I'm really talking about his robust moral fiber and deep empathy for the human race. Sometimes we stray, but Kaufman is our moral compass. He rights the ship."

The crowd let out a polite *"awww."* All eyes burned on Kaufman, who struggled to mask the disgust on his face. Did Milos really think he could flatter and cajole him into submission?

"You bastards better not try to steal him," Milos snickered. The plutocrats let out a nervous chuckle, as some had already been plotting to poach Kaufman. "To ensure that doesn't happen and to keep his unrivaled brain power in the Jupiter Fund family, I'm offering Kaufman a big promotion."

Milos stepped offstage and marched right at Kaufman. A hush befell the crowd. The traders clenched their fists in jealousy. Carrie cooed and squeezed him tighter. She fantasized about their future together. Kaufman felt dizzy, and disgust now consumed every last cell in his body. How could this guilty, decadent Soviet collaborator be so self-assured, so proud of himself, when all he did was harm?

"Kaufman, how would you like to be my right hand man, my chief innovation officer, my likely successor?" The last part elicited a great hush, as if all the oxygen had been sucked out of the place. Milos shoved the microphone in Kaufman's face.

"Go fuck yourself."

The crowd erupted in gasps and gossip. Milos flushed crimson in anger and shame. Carrie disengaged herself from Kaufman's arm and inched toward the other traders.

Kaufman stormed off, leaving the Vulture's Feast in uproar.

Shivering Kaufman slogged a couple miles to the train station, in the dead of night. The streets were barren and eerily quiet. He knew he'd never work on Wall Street again. In fact, Milos could probably have him blackballed from just about any job. He might not even be allowed to squirt guacamole from a caulking gun at Taco Bell. Kaufman didn't care.

No trains would arrive until morning and all the taxis in Westchester were tied up at Milos' estate. Kaufman reclined on a bench in the station and slowly drifted off to sleep. His life may have hit rock bottom, but at least he'd finally slipped his golden handcuffs.

His phone vibrated in his pocket and he jolted halfway back to consciousness. Which Sterling lackey was going to chew him out? He didn't recognize the number.

"Hello," he croaked.

A bored operator informed him: "I've got a 'See-boo' calling collect from The Democratic Republic of the Congo. Do you accept the charges?"

Kaufman assumed he was dreaming, but his heart still soared.

33

For the first time since starting on Wall Street, Kaufman flew coach. He was perfectly content to binge on over-salted peanuts, crammed between a doughy woman with her crying baby and a fidgeting, broad shouldered man with his elbow lodged in Kaufman's ribs. The flight was slow and turbulent, with staticy in-flight movies and a pressurized cabin recycling passengers' collective body odor. Kaufman was stripped of his empowered jetsetter status and willingly accepted his new place as a common prole. He had to carefully conserve his capital, since he wasn't sure how he'd ever make more. But he had never been more excited in his life.

His exhilaration was short lived.

Kaufman was stunned by the massive throngs of crushed, starving humanity swarming the refugee camp. He flashed his papers to a blue-helmet and passed through the barbed gate, clutching a cardboard box against his chest. He sensed that he was crossing the threshold into a new chapter of his life. At what point could he ever leave this place? Even if he spent his every waking moment trying to help, he might still accomplish nothing. He could hand over every penny he had and it would all just disperse so thinly among the needy, into an ineffectual mist. The want in this camp alone seemed insurmountable, so what would become of victims all over world? There were seven billion human beings packed around the planet and Kaufman reasoned that roughly half of them were screwed. From what he had seen of people, it was their intrinsic nature to either exploit or to look the other way.

The harried aid workers directed Kaufman toward his goal. As he pushed past destitute masses, many grabbed at his box. They were accustomed to fight for every supply cache, aid package and scrap of food. It was a matter of survival – there was never enough to go around. Kaufman had to charge past them to keep his gifts intact.

Sebu's camp duties included teaching the younger children in one of the "education tents," arranged in endless rows sprawling across the hard, flat dirt. There weren't nearly enough teachers, so knowledge trickled from a few trained educators, to the smartest children, all the way down the chain to the kindergarteners. By the time it reached them, some of the facts were distorted and misconstrued.

Sebu pointed to sentences scrawled on a dusty blackboard and his former soldiers listlessly read aloud.

"John plays ball. Mary jumps rope," the boys droned, clearly bored out of their minds.

"Sorry to interrupt." Kaufman peeked inside. Their spirits instantly lifted, the children leapt out of their seats and mobbed their lost friend with hugs.

"I brought a surprise." He opened his box and revealed the green, Ubuntu laptops specifically designed for third world children.

They regarded the bright plastic boxes with curiosity. Kaufman hoped they would treasure these tools the same way they had clung to their assault rifles. They would have to if they wanted to avoid being robbed by their campmates.

"Ever wonder where all that coltan goes?" Kaufman tapped a computer with his index finger, then handed one to each child.

The children's faces lit up as they heard the chimes of their booting computers.

"I won't lie to you," Kaufman leveled with them. "As we've all learned firsthand, the game is rigged and the odds are lousy. But maybe if you work ten times harder than the next guy, you might have a prayer." They didn't quite follow. They were all frantically exploring their electronic novelties, making their first contact with a digital interface.

"These machines aren't just for games. They won't solve all your problems, but they do connect you to the rest of humanity. And that connection brings opportunity."

The orphans betrayed a glimmer of hope. They still thought they were playing with toys, but Kaufman knew better. Each child held a portal to the outside world.

Kaufman sat with Sebu on discarded crates near the tumultuous intake line, eating gruel and watching the daily bustle. They idly chatted as fresh refugees poured in, hungry and exhausted, at the ends of their ropes. Some were already fighting for their share of the scraps, while others hardly had the strength to breathe. The multinational aid workers processed them with a combination of compassion and cold efficiency – they had to harden their bleeding hearts or they'd burn out before they could make the slightest dent in the gaping void of need.

Kaufman was so proud to hear the story of Sebu's daring ruse. Strategy prevailed over brute force. They caught up on old times, because even a couple months felt like eons, given their stormy recent lives.

"I never thought I'd miss this slop. What's it made of, anyway?" Kaufman sniffed his gruel.

"Corn husks and gunpowder."

Kaufman believed him for a second and Sebu couldn't help but laugh at the look on his face. But soon Sebu's melancholy crept back.

"My friend, why are you here? Haven't you had enough of this place?"

"I've had more than enough," Kaufman shrugged.

Sebu furrowed his brow. "I know I should just be grateful to be alive, but I'm not. I lost everyone. I thought once Makanga was dead, I'd feel better. But I don't."

Kaufman scrambled for some reassuring pleasantry, but he knew there was nothing to say. Sebu had no use for platitudes. Kaufman hugged his little friend. Sebu forced back tears.

They sat in silence for several minutes, watching the bent and broken shapes slump through the gateway to their salvation – or rather subsistence.

A scorched bus, perforated with bullet holes, sputtered to a halt outside the wire, coughing up its batch of wretched voyagers. They hobbled to the back of the line.

"They just keep coming," Sebu sighed.

"We should recruit that guy for our basketball team." Kaufman pointed to one of the taller men, slouching despondently at the end.

Sebu gasped. His hands trembled.

Kaufman was bewildered.

"I can't believe it," Sebu whispered in shock.

"Don't get your hopes up yet. He looks a little clumsy."

Sebu watched the last girl slink out of the bus, with a hangdog look and a thousand yard stare. His face illuminated with joy.

"Sister!" He cried out, tears already flowing down his cheeks like a waterfall. He sprinted to her, but she didn't recognize him at first.

She looked him up and down in utter disbelief and suddenly she too broke down in happy, sobbing convulsions. They fell into a long embrace.

Kaufman's jaw dropped. Could something good have actually come of this wretched place?

Sebu flicked his sister's ear, like he used to tease her in their stolen childhood. She lovingly swatted his hand away.

He led her to meet Kaufman, who cracked a hopeful smile. Their stories would continue, tomorrows entwined.

Acknowledgements

I am forever grateful to my parents for their undying love and support and for encouraging me in all pursuits, creative and otherwise.

Thanks to the Montag Press team for seeing value in this story. Eagle-eyed editor Nicholas Morine helped trim the fat and punch up the action. Publisher Charlie Franco's diligence and operational acumen saw the project through from a doc file to a fully realized book. Cover designer Niall Gray and illustrator Garrett Kohanek distilled the story's essence into visual form. Fellow Montag authors Marcin Dolecki, David Massengill and David Mathew were so generous with their consideration of the novel and with their advance praise.

The now-defunct Triggerstreet Labs online community helped me develop the story, back when it only existed in screenplay form.

Writers Justin Slosky and Shanna Green provided both their invaluable friendship and critical feedback on the rough draft of the novel.

I am so humbled and thankful to be born into a free society, with access to education, public libraries and the internet. Sadly, many are not afforded these great privileges.

Michael G. Keller is an award-winning filmmaker whose work has screened at festivals around the world, on cable television and Netflix. He has created content from sunny Hollywood, California to even sunnier Mumbai, India. *Toy Soldiers* is his first novel. He intends to direct the film adaptation.

www.MichaelGKeller.com